WITNESS

L.A. Gilbert

Dreamspinner Press

Published by
Dreamspinner Press
4760 Preston Road
Suite 244-149
Frisco, TX 75034
http://www.dreamspinnerpress.com/

This is a work of fiction. Names, characters, places and incidents either are the product of the author's imagination or are used fictitiously, and any resemblance to actual persons, living or dead, business establishments, events or locales is entirely coincidental.

Witness
Copyright © 2010 by L.A. Gilbert

Cover Art by Anne Cain   annecain.art@gmail.com
Cover Design by Mara McKennen

All rights reserved. No part of this book may be reproduced or transmitted in any form or by any means, electronic or mechanical, including photocopying, recording, or by any information storage and retrieval system without the written permission of the Publisher, except where permitted by law. To request permission and all other inquiries, contact Dreamspinner Press, 4760 Preston Road, Suite 244-149, Frisco, TX 75034
http://www.dreamspinnerpress.com/

ISBN: 978-1-61581-424-4

Printed in the United States of America
First Edition
April, 2010

eBook edition available
eBook ISBN: 978-1-61581-425-1

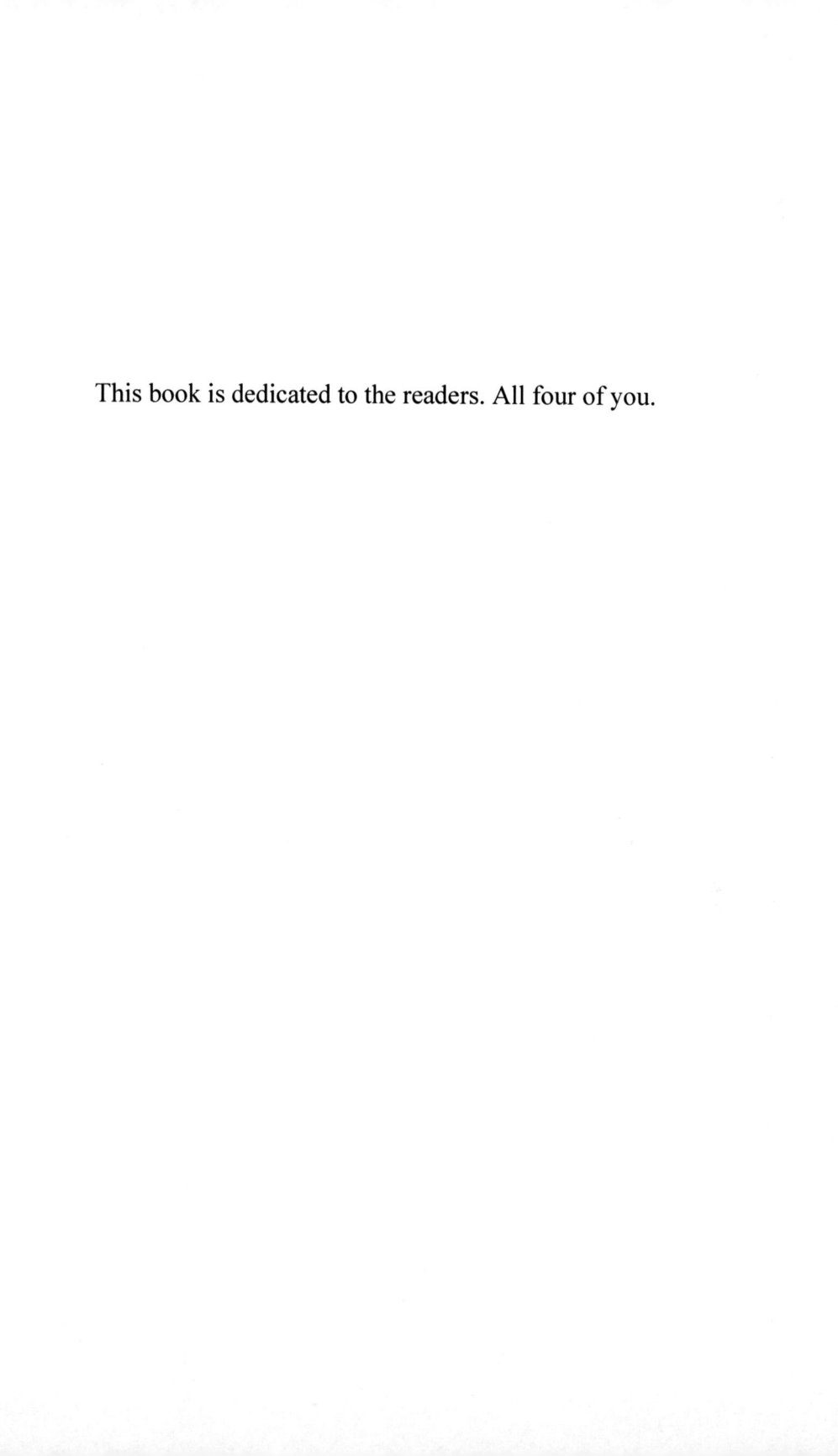

This book is dedicated to the readers. All four of you.

Witness

CHAPTER 1

WITH a small sigh, Ben reached over blindly to turn off his clock radio. He had been more or less awake for some time, dozing lightly, waiting for the annoying chatter of traffic news and weather reports to tell him it was time to get up and get ready for work. Pulling back the duvet, he sat up and swung his legs over the side of the bed. Rubbing his face briskly and giving his stubble a scratch, he yawned widely and stretched the kinks out of his neck.

He made his way over to the window, leaning his hands on the sill as he looked up at the sky to contemplate his options. It didn't look like it would snow.

"A quick run, or a go at the weights?" he asked himself.

The weather report had said brisk and then cold with a chance of sunshine. Despite it being far too early for sunshine, he chose to go for a quick run. He loved how fresh the air smelled first thing; there was no better way to wake up. And anyway, he knew he'd hit the weights in the evening after work.

"Once or twice around the park, then."

Boycotting the shower and pulling out a pair of sweats, T-shirt and a warm sweatshirt, he made his way down the stairs and to the front door, where he crouched to tie the laces to his running shoes. Pulling one leg up at a time to touch his heel to the back of his thighs, he deemed himself loose enough and, locking the door behind him, set out at a jog down the quiet street.

At six-thirty on a January morning, it was indeed brisk. He loved Seattle; he didn't think he'd likely ever move. Knowing a city inside out made a guy feel safe and in turn protective. Running this more-than-familiar route required no thinking, and with his guard down, his feet could just eat up the pavement. Capitol Hill was a good neighborhood, home to good people.

His breath misted in front of him as he picked up the pace; this was his favorite time of day. The park was quiet and empty, only the sounds of birds stirring could be heard. He made his second lap around the park, pulling his hands up into his sleeves when his fingers began to numb. He should have worn his gloves.

Ambling to a walk as he approached the house he had lived in for the majority of his thirty-four years, he wiped the sweat from his brow and stopped to stretch his legs before going inside. He took a few gulps from a bottle of water, then placed it back in the large fridge before reaching for the milk.

He shed his sweatshirt and set the milk, a bowl, and his favorite cereal down on the table, and pulled back a chair to sit. His breathing nearly normal again, he paused and ran a finger over the blue swirling design on the bowl. He'd eaten out of this same bowl as a child. He smiled fondly for a moment and then filled the bowl generously.

He looked around the kitchen as he chewed. It was a spacious kitchen, and so quiet, but he had grown used to it. If he closed his eyes, he could imagine hearing his father tinkering about, making coffee for himself and telling his son to hurry with his breakfast. They had always been in a rush in the mornings, despite waking at the crack of dawn. His father would get him up out of bed early, but then they would usually get to talking and end up scrambling to get out the door on time. Whether they'd be chatting about school or last night's game, they would always be surprised to see that they were running late.

He was in no rush now. Thanks to his dad, he'd never really been one to sleep in. Lately his days were pretty much the same: get up, lift weights or go for a run, go to work, come home, eat, either fit in a little

Witness

cardio or go at the weights again before settling in for the night with a book or in front of the TV.

Of course, occasionally he would deviate from his routine to make a trip out to a bar or club, despite not really being a huge fan of either. But everyone needed a little company now and then, didn't they? His choice of company tended to lean toward the male variety, not something he had ever hidden, but also not something he chose to advertise. A little anonymous sex was needed every so often, when porn and his hand no longer did the trick. So he would hook up occasionally, and though not always satisfying, it scratched an itch.

That was the way it went. He wasn't unhappy; he was simply a creature of habit. And at that moment another little creature of habit interrupted his musings with a soft mew.

"Hey, sweetheart."

Putting his bowl in the sink, he wiped his mouth with the back of his hand, and crouched to pick up the scruffiest, most ridiculous-looking cat ever. She was also the sweetest little thing he'd ever known.

"You want your breakfast too, huh?"

Loud purring answered him. He tucked her under one arm as he scratched the top of her head. He'd learned not to feel silly about talking to his cat soon after adopting the odd little stray.

He'd named her Muddles. She had a line that could have been drawn on with a ruler that went down the center of her little face, the left of it a patchy ginger, the right completely black. With long fur that always looked a mess, she looked every bit the stray, save for the red collar she wore with a little fish-shaped name plate that said otherwise. He'd found the grubby little fur ball in his yard while trimming his mother's bushes. She'd been tiny and pathetic looking, and he'd loved her immediately.

"Tuna today, Mud." He shook the packet of cat food and ripped open the top, filling her bowl. "Better you than me."

She didn't seem to mind, however, and hungrily began to stuff her face, purring the entire time, jelly attaching itself to her whiskers. Wiping his hands down his thighs, he grabbed his discarded sweater and headed upstairs for a shower.

Stuffing his clothes into the hamper, he pulled back the shower curtain and stepped under the warm spray. He dipped his head and sighed as the warm water ran over his scalp and down his broad back. He ran his hands through his hair, completely wetting it, and then reached for the shampoo. Lathering himself, he allowed his hands to wander lower until he cupped his heavy balls. He contemplated jerking off, his dick showing some interest, but decided he didn't have the time after taking that second lap around the park.

Rinsing off, he climbed out of the shower, grabbed a towel, and wrapped it around his trim waist. He wiped the bathroom mirror clear, and picked up his razor. He'd been shaving since he was sixteen—he'd needed to. Every morning without fail, there would be a light scruff. He didn't mind it, had even been told it was attractive, but it wouldn't do for an officer to look disheveled.

He smiled a small, melancholy smile. He remembered his father showing him how to shave for the first time, his dad's hands guiding his slowly over his chin, and then quickly swishing it clean in the sink before repeating the action. His father had been gone three years now, and he still found it hard to believe that he would never see the old man again. Ben applied the cream and scraped it gently away with his razor, an action that barely required any concentration after so many years. Sighing, he wiped any remaining foam from his chin, and looked at his reflection.

He didn't dislike how he looked; he knew he was handsome in a way, though he didn't see anything particularly striking. With short, black hair, a strong jaw, a straight nose, pale lips, and watery blue eyes, he guessed he didn't look bad, but nothing to write home about. He tensed his chest for a moment, not admiring, just looking to see if the extra ten pounds weight he'd been lifting had made any difference. He looked about the same, he decided. Broad shoulders, firm pecs covered in a light dusting of dark hair, and hard abs. He rolled his eyes at his reflection, feeling stupid for checking himself out. His only goal was to maintain a healthy lifestyle, and the workouts felt good. Not to mention that his job required him to be in good physical health. But mostly, he refused to watch what he ate. He loved food—and loved to cook—so the trade off was a lot of exercise. He didn't even own a set of scales.

After running a towel roughly over his hair, he dropped it into the hamper, along with the one around his waist. He took his uniform out of his closet, running his hand down the front of the shirt before laying it on the bed. Pulling out underwear and socks, he got himself ready for work.

Uniform on, belt, gun and cuffs attached, he pulled on his jacket and crouched again, dangled his keys in front of Muddles for a minute, and gave a small grin as she rolled onto her back to bat at the clinking metal. Stepping over her, he made his way to the door, pausing only for a second to glance at a framed photo of his father in uniform before heading off for another day.

REECE came awake with a start, his alarm blaring obnoxiously.

"Argh, shut *up*."

He sat up and reached for the damn thing, jabbing at the off button and shaking the shit out of it. Eventually it stopped, and with a groan he laid back across his pillows. It took only a few seconds for something to register, and he sat back up with a start, looking at the little red numbers that indicated that he should have left for work ten minutes ago.

"Shit!"

He leaped out of bed and ran straight to the bathroom, muttering the entire time.

"Fucking alarm, can't wake me up when I tell it to, oh no. Has a mind of its fucking own, doesn't it, gets me up when it's good and ready and not a minute before...."

He probably should have skipped the shower, as late as he was, but he'd been surprisingly tired last night and had fallen straight into bed without bathing first. Considering what he'd been doing all day yesterday, and what he'd be doing again today, he really did need one. Working downtown saw to that. He was clean in a record-breaking amount of time, and quickly brushed his teeth, barely glancing in the mirror. He knew what was there: shaggy brown hair, kind of scruffy but in an oddly appealing way—he hoped. Warm brown eyes, cheeky grin, lean body—so it fucking should be—and an eagerness to get on with life that sometimes made him appear younger than he actually was. As it stood, he was twenty-nine, approaching the big Three-O, and not looking forward to it one damn bit.

"A bike messenger at nearly thirty, way to go, Reece. And you wonder why you're single."

Of course, he wasn't *just* a bike messenger, and that wasn't what he wanted to be. It just paid the bills and had the small advantage of keeping him in shape; Lord knew he hated working out in his free time.

He was a freelance photographer. He advertised in the local papers, though it didn't seem to do him much good. Reece's Family Portraits. He'd position whiney little kids and screaming babies into a pose that resembled something adorable, take the shot, and then develop them in the nearest print lab. Again, not exactly what he wanted to be doing, but it was closer to professional photographer than bike messenger, at least. Truth was, he'd be most content to take pictures of mountains, lakes, pyramids... hell, the ducks down at the fucking park would do. But financial security was hard to come by, so adding to his portfolio (a portfolio he allowed himself to be proud of) was strictly reserved for his own free time, something else that was hard to come by.

Witness

He glanced quickly through his organizer as he dressed in a rush, looking to see if he had any bookings coming up, and sighed at the blank pages.

You'll get by.

Nothing but his standard, boring as fuck nine-to-five job for the moment, then. Luckily his boss was a darling, *and* his best friend. So he could take a day off work at short notice when these miraculous bookings did actually happen.

He was hungry but had no time to eat; he'd have to nab a pretzel on the way to his first drop or something. He loved food. He couldn't cook for shit, but could eat like a pro. Lucky for him, his vain ass had a quick metabolism.

You're not vain, you're single and a fucking bike messenger, add fat onto that and you'll die alone for sure.

He dashed back into his room, remembering at the last moment to feed his fish. Darren, his good buddy and boss, had bought the fish for him on his last birthday. Reece had joked at the time that a sweater from Gap would have sufficed, but he loved the little sucker—mostly because he hadn't killed it yet. He'd named it Wesley Snipes. Wesley Snipes the fish, because anyone could tell by looking at it that this was one badass fish—fucking *huge*, gold with a black tail and a little castle that it enjoyed knocking over.

Fish fed, he hefted his bike out of the narrow corridor of his cramped apartment, and set it aside so he could quickly ransack his tiny kitchen for wherever he'd left his keys.

"Gotcha!"

Stuffing them into his pocket, he pushed his bike to the door, pausing to jot down a note on a pad he kept beside his phone. The list of things he needed to buy—but as of yet could not quite afford—was getting longer and longer. He scribbled beneath where he'd written "new bike."

"Buy new... non-shit alarm clock."

Picking up his bike, he pushed it out of the door and locked up. The elevator was, of course, not working, had, in fact, never worked in the ten years—ten fucking years—he'd lived there.

Hefting the bike frame onto his shoulder—not exactly comfortable but at least the repetitive action afforded him arms that no longer resembled spaghetti—he made his way carefully down the stairs to begin another day of delivery and dodging traffic.

BEN held back a sigh. *Bickering couples should not be allowed to dial 911.* He stood in the apartment of a couple who had been screaming up a storm, over what he gathered so far was the woman's son-of-a-bitch husband's infidelity. She'd thrown half his shit out onto the street, and then gone to the kitchen for a knife. Or at least what the guy who had then promptly called the police had described as a knife. From where he was standing, this "huge fucking knife" looked a lot like an average-size potato peeler.

"Miss, please put down the, uh... potato peeler."

Had he ever had to say anything so ridiculous?

"What? You gonna *shoot* me?!" The woman cried.

"Not over a potato peeler, no." He wished he could stop saying "potato peeler."

"It looked like a knife when she came at me with it," the husband said.

Too right you should look embarrassed, you cheating dick. Ben exchanged a look of strained patience with the other officer who had joined him on the domestic call. He was a good guy, name of Brown, a young guy, new to the force, who apparently had a hard time keeping a

Witness

straight face when the guy—who was in his boxers and nothing else—flinched every time the woman moved or gestured with the "weapon."

"Miss, I don't want to have to arrest you over a... over *that*"—he nodded toward the peeler—"and I appreciate that you're very upset right now, but that isn't going to make anything better." He approached her slowly with a hand outstretched, gently touching her elbow. "Can we sit down, just for a minute?"

She seemed to calm under his touch and offered the peeler to him without a second thought. "Like I could hurt him with this. What am I gonna do, peel him?"

He guided the sniffling woman to the couch, exchanging a glance with Brown, who was speaking now to the husband, urging him to put some clothes on.

"My clothes are out in the fucking *street*—"

Ignoring the man's whining, Ben turned back to the middle-aged woman before him. She looked heartbroken.

"You realize if he asks to press charges, you'll have to come with us."

She shrugged, that small defeated gesture earning her his sympathy. "I'm sorry you were called, I didn't know he'd do that. It was just a vegetable peeler."

He bit back a small smile. "Yeah, not the most heroic of guys you got there."

She turned teary eyes to him, her chin trembling. Unconsciously he put a gentle arm around her shoulders. "He slept with my sister. Can you believe that?" she asked quietly.

He sighed, and replied to her in a quiet voice for her ears only. "I'm tempted to give you this back." He nodded toward his hand.

That earned him a small watery laugh. He'd do what he could. Make sure his report (if it came to that) read that she had not had a knife, and had not been trying to attack him, only scare him.

"Jenkins?"

Ben looked up at the mention of his name. Brown, who stood with a sheepish looking, still half-naked man behind him, seemed to have the situation under control.

"He doesn't want to press charges."

He heard the woman sigh in relief.

"The least you could do, if you ask me." His words were not directed at his partner. "Do one of you have somewhere else you could stay tonight, at least until you've both cooled off?"

"I'll go," the guy muttered.

"To her?" The woman broke down crying.

Ben cleared his throat uncomfortably; he hated these calls. Fortunately, his radio chose that moment to crackle to life. He shared a brief look with Brown before nodding and heading out into the hall to take it.

It turned out to be another call. He looked back into the apartment and briefly explained to Brown.

"Go, I got this," Brown said.

He thanked Brown and left. The domestic no longer needed two officers on location. He felt for the woman, but there was nothing more he could do.

He liked Brown. He wondered if they'd end up partnered together. He'd been a cop for a number of years now. His old partner, Ted Adams, had been wounded three months ago, and it didn't seem like he planned on coming back. The thought made Ben a little sad, but Adams was a good fifteen years his senior, and had lost some of his passion for the job. It made it easy for Ben to understand why he might take worker's comp and early retirement from the force. He'd earned it; he'd have a limp for the rest of his life and he had scared the shit out of his wife to boot.

Ben made a mental note as he climbed back into his vehicle to pay his old partner a visit soon. While he'd grown used to riding alone the past couple of months, it could get a little boring. Well, either boring or dangerous. Brown would make a good partner. He'd just have to wait and see what happened there.

Speaking over the radio, he made his destination known and pulled away. Hopefully this call would be the last of his shift.

REECE groaned as he all but dropped his bicycle in his short hallway, pushing the door shut behind him with his foot. What a day. He'd made thirteen drops and his ass was killing him—and *not* in a good way.

Darren had been fine with him, as always. Well, he'd greeted him with a "Where the fuck have you been?" before shoving his first delivery of the day into his arms.

"You'd better have been getting laid, you know no other excuse is acceptable."

"I agree, but alas, it was the alarm clock from hell. It wants you to fire me."

"It may just get its wish if you keep this up."

"But Darren," he'd said, giving his best helpless itty bitty kitty look and blinking sadly at the man, "you know I'd be destitute without this shitty job."

"So you'd think you'd try a little harder to keep it."

"I'd have to pedal my ass on the streets. Sell my bicycle helmet. Give blow jobs for change!"

"Oh, like you wouldn't love giving head for a living."

"Not to married, balding, fat businessmen I wouldn't."

Darren had just laughed and said, "Then I suggest you get going. Go!"

He'd been pushed out the front door, his best friend grinning at him affectionately, but his day had gone downhill from there. He hated office drops. He hated standing there in his cycling gear, waiting for a signature while successful businessmen in their successful businessmen suits strode past him looking all superior and shit. He was well aware that it was most likely all in his head—that they in fact didn't even notice him and that it was his own hang-ups that made him think that way. Still. It wasn't a great feeling. And today he'd had some posh asshole, all handsome and distinguished looking, in a suit that probably cost more than he earned in a month, yell at him in front of a foyer full of people for something that wasn't even his fucking fault. He just delivered the goddamn packages; he didn't know what was in them. That wasn't his *or* Darren's responsibility. The day hadn't really gotten any better after that, but at least it was done now.

He leaned over the fridge door, gazing mournfully at the near empty shelves.

"Cereal, it is. I should probably learn to cook one of these days."

He forced down a bowl of cereal, looking back at the fridge and willing it to fill with actual food. It wasn't that he couldn't afford the groceries; he could buy himself food at the very least. He was just too goddamn tired to attempt to cook anything.

He had to face it: he was getting older. Gone, for the most part anyway, were the nights spent dancing till three in the morning and picking up some guy he'd probably never see again. It bothered him, but not in the obvious way. Everyone eventually got older and he wasn't ashamed to be turning thirty soon, he certainly wouldn't lie about his age. He'd simply envisioned his life being a little different by now. His career was supposed to have taken off; he was supposed to be living in at least a semi-decent apartment.

He looked at the place that had been his home since he was nineteen and winced. Apart from the photography on the walls, his apartment could still be mistaken for student digs. He felt a lump develop in his throat. If he were to be honest, he felt a little embarrassed, perhaps a touch ashamed.

Darren was always telling him to go easier on himself. That at least he was out there, trying to make his way under his own steam. Never mind that if his friend hadn't gotten him his job, he'd probably be stuck stocking shelves or working in fast food.

"I trust you," Darren had said, "and you look good in cycling pants." Those had been Darren's reasons for talking to his then-boss and getting him the gig, without an interview, without him even having to *ask*. Damn, he loved that guy. He took a deep breath and let it out slowly. He owed it to his friend to keep trying. He'd get there.

"You'll get there," he murmured quietly.

After feeding Wesley again (that fish ate a *lot*), he forced himself into the shower. Taking it slowly this time, he even relaxed enough to take himself in hand. He imagined feeling a solid weight moving above him, between his thighs, his hands running over a broad, hard back down to a trim waist he'd grip as it ground into his body. It wasn't long before he was shuddering and rinsing off. At least now if he were late again, he could run straight for the door.

Sliding into bed and then pulling out his plain black journal from his nightstand, he started to make one of his lists. He hated these lists, but he'd never been able to break the habit, not in ten years. Eventually, he placed the journal back in the nightstand, reached for his alarm clock and regarded it coldly.

"Now when I set you to seven a.m., you are going to go off at seven—*fucking*—a.m. If you don't, then I'm smashing the shit out of you."

Sliding down between his sheets, he thought for a moment how it might be nice to be falling asleep beside someone right about then, and drifted off.

BEN laid back on the bench press, his hands reaching up to grip the bar comfortably. He took a few steady breaths before lifting it with a grunt. Lowering it to his chest, he held his breath as he pushed back up, exhaling as his arms straightened.

He repeated this process and other exercises with the weights for a good hour before calling it quits. Grabbing a small towel, he wiped his brow, the back of his neck and then sent a quick swipe over his chest. He panted a little and walked around in slow circles with his head tilted back to cool down.

He hated going to bed sticky, so he grabbed a quick shower before climbing into bed. He sighed, realizing he was feeling a little lonely. Perhaps he was due a trip out to the bars.

He'd only been home long enough that afternoon to change out of his uniform before heading out again. One of the guys at work had invited a bunch of them over to watch a baseball game on the flat screen. It had generally been an okay evening, despite baseball not really being his thing. He was a football man, personally. It had been the chatter that had left him feeling a little melancholy.

Chatter about their families, wives, their kids. All the things he didn't have and for the most part never would. Of course he wasn't the only single guy there; it just felt that way at times. He had the impression that it was a lot easier for them to meet women—with the intention of more than a hookup—than it was for him to meet men. Perhaps a trip to the bars wouldn't do the trick this time. Bars were good for meeting guys for casual sex, but not so much for dating.

Did he want to date again? It had been a long time. He'd dated casually before, but it never really seemed to work out. Either his job

Witness

got in the way, or he did. He remembered the last guy he'd try to date, Jason, complaining that he was too boring. That had hurt more than he wanted to admit. So he wasn't really one for going out *every* night. So he preferred evenings curled up together on the couch. That didn't mean he was boring. It just meant that he preferred quality time alone with his man. It meant that they hadn't been right for each other. Nothing more.

Sighing, Ben rolled over and patted the side of the bed when he saw a tail peeking over the edge. Muddles jumped up, pushing her head into his hand and curling right up against his side.

"I got you, don't I, girl?"

Thing was, it didn't really seem enough anymore.

CHAPTER 2

BEN looked up at the building. Not the flashiest of apartment blocks, but he'd seen worse. He buzzed next to where "Roger" had been written in what seemed a shaky hand. The call he'd answered had been from a Roger Townsend, an elderly gentleman, said to be the owner of the building that he rented out to various tenants. Ben let out a surprised little laugh when he spotted the smiley face drawn next to the name.

"Okay, definitely an odd one. Sweet, but odd."

He heard a crackle, and then said gentleman's voice blaring out over the speaker. He jumped a little and blinked in surprise. He wouldn't have put that voice with the spindly handwriting.

"This is Officer Jenkins."

"Yes?"

Instead of sighing in frustration as he usually might, he smiled a little.

"You called the police, Mr. Townsend. About a noise coming from your apartment. You thought you had an intruder?" The dispatcher had told the guy to leave his apartment and wait for the officer; he should be down here waiting to let Ben in.

"Oh yes! I'll buzz you in and meet you on the stairs!"

This time Ben couldn't hold back a small groan as he pushed open the door. The department was well used to these types of calls.

Witness

They got a dozen or so every day from the elderly community, startled by this or that. Of course some of them were legitimate, but nine times out of ten it was over something that didn't really need a cop's attention. He'd even answered a call once from a woman who'd reported a burglary, but had in fact just needed a light bulb changed. Her defense had been that they wouldn't have come if she'd told the truth. He'd changed the bulb and left.

"Hello, Officer."

Ben actually winced at the volume of his voice. Who would have thought such a small old man could make so much noise? Climbing the stairs to the first floor, he understood better when he spotted two hearing aids.

"Good evening, sir." He tried to speak as clearly as possible, and a touch louder than usual. He hoped he didn't sound patronizing. He pulled the man gently aside, away from his door, and Roger frowned at him.

"I'll need you to stand away from your apartment as I check for intruders, sir."

"Oh, I see. It's coming from the bathroom. A splashing sound."

Now even more than before, he doubted that there was an intruder. But if there was one, then he was pretty sure they'd had fair warning if Mr. Townsend had made the call from his own apartment.

"I think they're using my bath!"

Ben bit back a smile; he'd still take every precaution, just in case there really was a burglar taking a bath in the old timer's place.

Out of habit more than anything, Ben put his hand over his gun, ready to pull it if needed, though he doubted very much that would happen. He made himself known, calling out toward the bathroom, where he could hear splashing and an odd buzzing noise.

Pushing the bathroom door open slowly, he found exactly what he expected: nothing. He followed the sound, and groaned aloud at seeing what it was. Not a minute later, he came back out into the hall, having taken a moment inside to compose himself first so that he wouldn't laugh and offend the strangely likeable old guy.

"Do you have them?" Roger's eyes, bright with excitement, met his, and he had to shake his head—almost apologetically—before revealing the culprit.

"Sir, your electric toothbrush had fallen into the toilet."

Why the guy even had one he didn't know, surely those were dentures.

"Oh."

And, bless him, he did look a little sheepish.

Just then a huffing, slightly breathless noise drew Ben's attention to the stairs, and the man ascending them. Ben stared.

A man carrying a bicycle over one shoulder was climbing the stairs toward them, and he was damned pretty. Ben's innate cop mentality of taking in a person's finer details kicked in: tousled brown hair, slim, lean build (definitely capable of pulling off a pair of cycling pants), perhaps two or three inches shorter than him, and quite obviously physically fit.

"Reece, hello, Reece!" Roger called, giving a wave as the guy—Reece, apparently—walked toward them.

"Rog, hey, buddy." Reece lowered the bike to the ground, his breath returning to normal, then frowned when he saw Roger standing beside a police officer. *Whoa.* Reece cleared his throat. *Never had a thing for uniforms before, but I most definitely wouldn't say no.* "Everything okay?" He looked between Roger and the officer. The oh-so-fuckable officer.

"There was thought to be a disturbance at this address, fortunately Mr. Townsend is fine. There's no problem." Seeing Roger hide the toothbrush in his cardigan pocket, Ben saw no need to go into details and embarrass him any further. He unconsciously gave Reece a once over. Those had to be the most gorgeous, big brown eyes Ben had ever seen.

Witness

"Oh, well, I'm glad. I'm Reece, Reece Withers." He held his hand out.

"This is Officer Jenkins," Roger offered.

"*Ben* Jenkins," Ben amended, clearing his throat, glad that the collar of his jacket would hide the flush creeping up his neck.

"Nice to meet you." Reece didn't let go of that strong hand and smiled warmly at Ben. The guy was big, kind of muscular looking—though it was difficult to tell under the jacket he was wearing—and had a very open, kind face. There was a hint of five o'clock shadow showing on his firm jaw, and he had pitch black hair and light blue eyes. Reece's perusal was interrupted, however, by Roger, God love him.

"Reece is a gay."

Ben blinked and looked back at Roger in surprise. Yes, he'd begun to sense that, but he wasn't used to hearing it put so bluntly. Particularly by a senior citizen with hearing aids. Ben eventually let go of the hand he held, feeling awkward with the old guy staring at them both. "I'm sorry?" he asked Roger.

"A—he's gay. He lives on my top floor, end of the hall," Roger repeated, making Reece laugh.

"Thanks, Rog." Reece smiled at Ben. He was a little disappointed. He'd thought maybe Officer Ben had been showing an interest in him; now he wasn't sure. Christ, his gaydar was for *shit*. "I'm thinking of getting some business cards printed up," he joked.

Ben laughed, but Roger looked confused.

"Gays do that now?"

Roger's question was so naïvely innocent, the old guy loved to think of himself as "enlightened" and was very proud of having a homosexual in his building. Reece couldn't help but tease. "Oh sure, I'm all out of them now, though."

Roger nodded as if this made perfect sense, and then his lined face lit up as a thought struck him. "Say, why don't you two come on in for a drink, perhaps a game of poker? It'll be just us fellas." Roger looked at Ben, "I always keep a little beer in the fridge for when Reece visits me."

Ben couldn't help but smile. Reece Withers must be a real nice guy. He was about to refuse when Roger disappeared into the apartment, returning seconds later with two beers, slightly out of breath from rushing. He'd see this sometimes, an elderly person who clearly craved company, and it always broke his heart a little.

"He just gets a kick out of the store clerk's face when they see a little old man waltz up to the counter with a six pack," Reece said to Ben.

Ben laughed but tilted his head apologetically at Roger. "I'm sorry, Mr. Townsend, but I'm still on duty."

"Oh, shame. Reece?"

"Tell you what," Reece said as he lifted the bicycle back up onto his other shoulder with a huff, "why don't I go get cleaned up and dump this thing, then I'll come back down and you can kick my ass at Go Fish?"

Definitely a nice guy, Ben decided.

"Excellent," Roger said, beaming.

"Well, I'd best be on my way," Ben said. He realized that if he didn't have to be on duty for a couple more hours that he might have liked a game of Go Fish with Roger and Reece.

"Oh, um…." Roger actually lowered his voice a little, to what would have passed for a normal volume. "I apologize if I've wasted your time."

"Not at all. You did the right thing. Better safe than sorry, right?"

"It was nice meeting you…." Reece offered his hand again, and keeping eye contact, decided to be daring, "…Ben."

Ben cleared his throat. "Yes, it was." He nodded, shook Reece's warm hand, and watched the good-looking man head toward the next staircase.

"Uh, wouldn't the elevator be easier?" He gestured to the old-fashioned elevator behind him.

Reece grinned. "Yeah, it probably would be." Reece looked back at Roger and asked loudly, "Don't you think, Roger?"

"I'll get to it, these things take time you know," Roger said as he backed into his apartment quickly and closed the door.

Reece laughed. "He's been saying that since I first moved in."

Ben smiled and nodded. "Well, I'll see you around." He wasn't sure why he'd said that.

"I hope so."

Ben blinked, nodded, and turned to walk down the stairs. It was only when he was back in the cruiser that he started to berate himself.

"You wanted to date again, a cute guy gives you all the signs, and you walk away. Good work, Jenkins."

He started the car and pulled away from the sidewalk. He thought about only one thing as he drove away: top floor, end of the hall.

WELL, damn. He couldn't have acted any more interested without embarrassing himself, surely? Reece watched Officer Handsome descend the stairs, and then with a sigh, made his way to his own apartment.

Putting down the bike, he wasted no time in climbing into the shower. He needed to wash the grime off of his skin. The sweat from rushing and being in the path of exhaust fumes all day accumulated and left him feeling less than fresh at the end of the day.

He winced. Ah. Of course. Of course he'd look a mess when meeting one of the hottest guys he'd seen in a long time. A *long* time. It wasn't natural for a gay man to go without sex for so long. It had been six months since his last encounter, which probably seemed alright to the average guy, but to a gay guy it was like dog years; you tripled it or something.

Reece shook his head at his internal ramble. He did talk some absolute crap sometimes. It was probably a good thing he hadn't gotten Ben's number. A guy like that? That gorgeous? He probably had them lining up around the corner for him. And Reece wasn't so good at detaching a good lay from a relationship. Or so he'd come to realize.

He stepped out of the shower; he didn't want to think about that. Frowning, he draped a towel around his trim waist and ran his fingers through his hair. He was almost grateful to hear the phone ring.

"Hello?"

"Hello, dear."

"Mom, hi. How've you been, how's Dad?"

"Your dad's just fine, aside from his back."

"It's still giving him some hassle, huh?"

"Well, he will insist on doing everything for himself at that workshop, never mind that he has staff to do it for him."

His father built furniture. Nothing outlandish or modern, but good sturdy furniture at a reasonable price. He'd started as some kind of apprentice in a similar role, and now, nearly thirty years later, he ran his own small business. He was a good guy.

"Well, that's Dad, isn't it."

"Hmm."

"And you, Mom? You doing okay?"

"Yes, sweetheart, thank you for asking. I was calling to see if we'd be seeing you any time soon; it's been a while since your last visit."

Witness

Reece smiled. His mother wasn't nagging, just checking up. And he appreciated it more than she probably knew. His relationship with his parents had never really been the same since he'd came out to them—since the accident. They weren't harsh or cruel, just a little more reserved around him. As if they were worried they'd say the wrong thing, like they didn't quite know the person their son had become when he'd turned eighteen and got his driver's license. That distance that sat between them, though at times inconsequential, hurt sometimes. They'd been really close when he was a kid, really happy, the four of them. Now it was only three, and he'd never really been able to broach the space between them that was Ryan's absence.

But they spoke once every fortnight or so, and he'd go visit on holidays and birthdays. He hadn't had them at his apartment since his early twenties; he was far too embarrassed of it. He wanted them to be proud, and as far as he knew, they were. They certainly seemed proud whenever he took his portfolio home with him; they didn't need to know that his job as a messenger was his main source of income. It was better to let them think it was the other way around, and that he only worked for Darren for the extra cash.

Just then there was a knock at the door. "Hang on one sec, Mom." He cradled the phone between his shoulder and neck as he tightened his towel, then held the phone to his chest and answered the door.

Roger stood there with a couple of beers (which Reece knew were just for him since the old man didn't drink—the big sweetie) and a pack of cards.

"Hey, Rog."

"Thought I'd save you the trip."

Reece smiled and waved him in. He felt a pang of affection for the guy; he'd obviously been downstairs waiting for him. He knew how much Roger liked the company ever since his wife passed a few years ago.

"Come on in and get comfy, help yourself to some tea or coffee. I've just got my mom on the line."

Roger nodded and headed into the kitchen.

"Reece?"

"Hey, Mom, sorry about that...."

"That's alright, do you have company? Who's Rog?"

Reece grinned. "Roger? He owns the building I live in?"

"Oh yes." There was a hint of disappointment in her voice. He'd never once brought someone home to meet his parents, and the fact that this bothered his mother reassured him at times.

"Listen, Mom, I should go, but I'll have a look at my diary and see what bookings I've got coming up. I'll give you a call later on in the week."

"All right. Oh, and will you bring your portfolio with you? We have new neighbors and your dad's made a new friend." The smile in his mother's voice was obvious. His dad really was kind of cute like that sometimes. "His name's Bill, and your father wanted to show him your work."

Reece felt a sudden lump form in his throat. For all they had been through, and despite any doubts he might feel about himself, he knew he had himself some real decent folks for parents.

"Sure, Mom." He knew his voice had gone soft. "Tell him I'd love to."

"Well, look after yourself, and call me soon."

"Will do, bye, Mom."

"Goodbye, dear."

He walked into the kitchen to see Roger sipping at his tea, a beer sitting opposite him on the table, with the cards between them.

"I'll just be a sec, Rog." He nodded toward his bedroom and went to get dressed. He felt a little better. He might not have achieved everything he had set out to yet, and he might not have a hot cop boyfriend, but he had some good people in his life.

Witness

BEN stood on the front porch, listening to dogs bark at hearing him knock, and the sound of twin nine-year-old girls rushing to the door. He couldn't help but smile.

"Hi, Ben!" Amy chirped

"Hey sugar, your mom around?"

"Hey, Ben!" called Tracey, who was trying to hold back one of their beagles. "Stop that, Chicken!"

Ben snorted. He loved that his ex-partner's daughters had chosen to name their two dogs Chicken Head and Cinderella. How freakin' cute was that?

"Ben, hi there."

That was Sharon, Ted's awesome wife. She had fire-red hair and the sweetest personality. Every time he visited, she insisted on sending him home with some form of food. Like being single *and* gay meant he was going to starve or something. She had no idea that he was actually a pretty good cook, but it didn't matter. She made really great raisin cookies that he *and* Muddles enjoyed. Weird cat.

"Hey, Sharon, let me give you a hand."

It looked like he'd come at a bad time. She had on an apron and one oven mitt. She was trying to pull back Cinderella as Tracey did the same with Chicken Head. Ben gave Chicken a quick ruffle as he took the dog's collar from Tracey and herded them inside.

"Hey, is that Ben I hear?"

"Yeah, honey, now get off your butt and come say hello. And get the girls cleaned up for dinner."

Ted appeared, looking a lot brighter than the last time Ben had seen him, which made him smile widely.

"Ted, you're looking good, man." He was delighted.

"Well, I won't be dancing the samba any time soon, but I'm feeling a lot more mobile, thanks."

"Look, I won't stay long," he said to both Ted and Sharon. "I just wanted to drop by and see how you were doing, old man."

"Old man," Ted huffed. This was a routine of theirs, something he still enjoyed. "Forty-nine is not as old as you think. You'll figure that one out when you get there yourself."

"Yeah, but you make it look old. Then again, that could be the cane."

Ted had been shot on one of their calls—their *last* call together. He needed a cane right now, but hopefully he would be rid of it in a month or so and have nothing more than a limp to show for his troubles.

"Ben, honey, there's enough for one more at the table. Stay and eat with us," Sharon said. In the same breath she turned to her husband and said, "Ted Adams, make yourself useful and get those girls cleaned up." The words were said with playfulness, but all the same Ted did as he was told, making Ben grin.

"What about it, sweetie? We're having casserole."

"Thanks, Sharon, but I can't. Got a… date. A date to get ready for." He wasn't quite sure where the lie had come from, but he did know that he'd forgotten to feed Muddles that morning and would be going home to one pissed kitty.

Ted was rounding his kids up the stairs, telling them to clean up as Sharon's eyes lit up with delight. "Oh, do tell. What's his name? How'd you meet?"

Ben smiled, feeling bashful, of all things. He'd known Sharon for as long as he'd known Ted. He'd liked her immediately, with her mother-hen nature and cheeky sense of humor. She was older than him, of course, close to Ted in age, but he'd always thought of her as a friend and even family, especially after his father had passed.

"Come on, details." She smiled and crossed her arms, waiting.

Witness

He only had to think for a second.

"His name's Reece, we... ran into each other at the store. Got talking, you know how it goes." Why he was saying all this, he wasn't quite sure.

"And...." she prompted. Ted limped back to her side, and she ushered them both to the kitchen so she could check the oven and Ted could sit at the table. Ben sat down at the table with him.

"And...." He looked at Ted, grinning.

"Oh, go ahead." Ted waved his hand in a dismissive motion. "Talk about men. The whole gay thing stopped making me blink like an owl years ago, thanks to you."

Ben and Sharon laughed. Older straight guys were always the ones to get the most weirded out about homosexuality. Though thinking that, Ben couldn't help but picture Roger Townsend, which led him right back to his original trail of thought.

"Well, he's pretty gorgeous, I gotta say."

"Yes, go on...." Sharon said.

Ben laughed. "Has being cooped up with this guy starved you for intelligent conversation or something?"

"I'd hardly call this intelligent conversation, but finish what you were saying," Ted said, much to Ben's surprise. His surprise must have been evident. "Come on, kiddo, even I'm interested. You've been on your own for too long, now; it's about time you got to dating again."

Even Sharon blinked in surprise, but then she smiled gently. Now Ben felt bad about lying in the first place.

"Well, um...." His mouth turned up at the corner. "He's cute, most definitely. Seemed a real sweet guy, funny too. And he's got the biggest—"

Ted cleared his throat, and Ben looked at him in exasperation.

"Brown eyes," Ben said clearly, grinning, making Sharon laugh. "As if I'd comment on his dick with your wife present, or you, for that matter."

Sharon laughed even louder, and Ted groaned.

"It's a first date, so... that's about it." He shrugged, feeling guilty for lying, and not even knowing why he had.

The sounds of the twins thundering down the stairs like miniature elephants brought that conversation to an abrupt halt, and Ben stood. "So I'd better be going. Glad to see you're doing better, Ted."

"I'll walk you to the car," Ted offered.

Ben would usually tell him not to bother, but he had the feeling Ted wanted to speak to him alone, so he said nothing. He bent down and kissed the girls goodbye, and even gave Chicken Head and Cinderella a quick pat.

"Bye, honey," Sharon called, already busy getting the girls seated.

Out at the car, Ted leaned against it for support. Ben waited patiently.

"I'm not coming back, Ben."

Ben nodded; he'd thought as much. He was disappointed, but completely understood.

"Maybe a desk job, maybe not. But definitely not active duty."

"Well, naturally, Ted, your leg...."

"Just don't want you to think I'm letting you down, kid."

"Aw, come on, Ted. I'm thirty-four, I'm a big boy. They'll partner me up with someone else."

"Yeah...."

Ben grinned. "I mean, I'll probably have to look after some clueless rookie, but it'll be alright. Sound familiar?"

Witness

Ted smiled, but then it faded. He sighed. "I gave Sharon the fright of her life, you know."

"I know."

"And we've got those girls to look after. You know, we never thought it'd happen for us." He shook his head, and Ben squeezed his shoulder. "But then those... beautiful little girls arrived. Let me tell how much of a shock that was," he said with a laugh, his eyes glistening. "Sharon, pregnant at thirty-nine. Scandalous!" He laughed again, then said gently, "A miracle is what it is, and I nearly lost it all, Ben."

"You don't have to explain a thing, Ted. I get it, I swear."

Ted took a deep breath, looked down to the ground and then back again, looking Ben right in the eye. "You're family. You got that? Family."

Ben blinked in surprise and then nodded, lost for words.

"I know you miss your daddy a great deal. He was a good man; I looked up to him a lot too. I was *his* young rookie, remember?"

Ben laughed, sounding a little strained, and nodded.

"What I'm trying to say," Ted said as he shuffled closer, "is that you've got us." He nodded to his house. "You ain't alone, buddy. I still got your back. And you don't need an excuse or an invite to come see us." He shoved his shoulder. "Alright?"

Ben ignored the manly shove and pulled Ted into a quick, gentle hug. Unable to speak, he nodded again.

"Now get going. You got that date, yeah?"

"Yeah."

Ben climbed into the car, watching Ted make his way back up to the porch before he pulled away. He quickly wiped the back of his hand over his eyes and sniffed loudly, clearing his throat and his vision. He hadn't been expecting that. It brought up things he preferred not to think about, such as the fact that he had no living family left. But it was good to know—what Ted had told him. He felt grateful for it.

As he drove up to his house—his big, empty house—he didn't feel quite as alone as he usually did when pulling up. But if he could change one thing, it would be to make his little lie a truth. He'd like to be going on a date tonight, instead of to bed, alone.

CHAPTER 3

BEN was relieved to be going home. His shift had ended earlier than usual today, and he was grateful. He slumped down into the driver's seat and ran a hand over his face; he was pretty sure he could feel the beginnings of a migraine. He'd go for a run tonight, a good long one, and clear his head.

He'd had one bad call after another. One woman in her late sixties had her purse snatched, and had been knocked over and hurt in the process. Not only had they not been able to catch the guy, but he'd learned later, when he went to the hospital to take her statement and get a better description, that the poor woman had died from the head wound she'd received.

Then he'd had some spoiled rich kid scream at him about his stolen car. It had quite literally taken all of his strength not to knock him out, particularly after having tried to find the family of the purse snatch victim—Emily Holden—so that he could give them the bad news, only to discover that she had lived all alone, with no family to speak of. That had resonated with him. In fact, it had hit him like a brick wall. It gave them a commonality he didn't want to think about.

All his other calls had felt insignificant in comparison, like this last one. He was parked outside of an office building. Someone had apparently been fired and not taken it well. Well, that was what *their* goddamn security guards were for, surely?

He just hadn't been able to shift what felt like a lead ball sitting in his stomach. It had been a long time since he'd felt this down. Sighing and rubbing his face again, he straightened his shoulders and started the engine. He would go see Ted. He knew without a doubt that Ted would understand, and that he'd feel better after having at least spoken about his day with someone else.

He threw a quick glance over his shoulder and put the car into reverse. He even managed a small smile knowing that this was just a funk, and that he didn't need an excuse or an invite to go see the guy, either. Those had been his words. Yeah, he was feeling a bit better at the prospect of seeing his pal and maybe getting a home cooked meal from Sharon—at least until he heard the sound of metal scraping under his back wheels.

He slammed his brakes immediately. With his pulse spiking and fearing the worst, he swung open his door to step out, only to nearly choke himself on his seatbelt. Unbuckling with a curse, he leapt from the car, already going for the radio on his shoulder in case an ambulance was needed.

Fortunately, after a quick scan, he could see that there were no mangled bodies lying anywhere, just a bicycle that had been completely destroyed under his back wheels. The front wheel and handlebars were bent all out of shape.

"Oh thank God," he said.

He knew he'd have some explaining to do to the owner, but as long as he hadn't hurt anyone, he didn't really care. He bent down and tried to pull the bike out. With a shimmy he managed to pull it free, probably damaging the underside of the car in the process, but what the hell. Couldn't really get any worse, now could it?

He frowned. Why did he recognize this bike? Did he even know anyone who owned one? Then it dawned on him.

"Oh fuck."

He figured it out right about the same time that the owner came out from the office building behind him. His shoulders actually hunched up in a wince when he heard his words repeated with slightly more gusto.

"Fuck!"

Ben turned to face an astonished Reece. Reece's eyes only widened on seeing who held his former bike.

"Reece—ah, Mr. Withers. I'm sorry, I can explain this."

Reece crossed his arms over his chest and raised his brows "Oh? Then please," he said, gesturing to the bike before crossing his arms again, "go ahead."

Ben licked his lips quickly, looking back at his car, down at the crumpled metal and rubber in his hands, then back to Reece. "I ran over your bike."

Reece would have laughed if he wasn't so pissed. "You don't say," he deadpanned.

Ben stepped closer, his expression sincere. "I am very sorry; I'll pay for a new one."

Reece breathed out heavily through his nose and let his arms swing down to his sides as he looked away for moment. Looking back at Ben, seeing the embarrassed flush creeping up the man's neck, his voice was far less aggressive when he spoke next. "You get that I'm a bike messenger, right?" He wanted to be annoyed; he *should* be. "Without a bike I'm just—that would make me a mail man."

"Again—" Ben started to say, but Reece interrupted him.

"And I don't drive. That was my only form of transport. Thank you."

Reece could see the guilt etched over that handsome face as the officer tried to think of something more to say. Reece felt his shoulders slump. "Oh, for God's sake. You could at least be a dick about this."

"What?"

"I'm trying to be all pissed off here and you're making it very difficult, looking all sorry and shit."

"I am sorry and shit. Look, just tell me what you want me to do to make this better."

A few crude thoughts came to mind, but Reece dismissed them; he still couldn't figure this guy out. He sighed and rubbed the back of his neck. "You could give me a ride. It's a bit of a long walk, you know?"

"Of course. Least I could do."

"Yeah tell me about it," Reece muttered. "Uh, don't bother with that." He pointed to the bike when Ben went to put in his car. "Give it here, there's no fixing that, it's down for the count. I think there's a dumpster around the corner somewhere."

"I'll do it."

Reece leaned against the side of the car as he watched Ben dispose of it. Shit. He couldn't afford a new one, but he didn't want this guy knowing that. He'd have to see if Darren had a spare.

He tilted his head to the side as he studied the cop's ass as he walked away. God, he could lick that man all over, he really could. Despite the fact that he'd just cost Reece his only form of transport in this city, he knew he'd still give the guy his number if he asked for it. How pathetic was that?

Ben was thinking differently, however. *There's no god damn way he'll date you now asshole. If wrecking his bike hadn't done it, then stammering your apologies like a loser would. Will this day never fucking end?*

Back at the car, they got in and drove in near silence. To say that it was uncomfortable for Ben was an understatement. He felt so embarrassed he couldn't think of a single damn thing to say to redeem himself.

Reece, however, was thinking that he'd already run into hunky Officer Ben twice, a third time didn't seem likely. They'd be arriving at his apartment in a few minutes, and he needed some indication, *something*, to tell him if Ben was a possibility or if he was just a nice guy, and Reece was barking up the wrong tree. Ben pulled up outside his building, and Reece ran his hand along the stitched detail of the car door.

"You know, not asking me for my number was forgivable, but then destroying my property... can't I get you arrested for that or something?" He smiled; he'd made it as light and teasing as possible, and he couldn't have been any clearer if he'd tried.

"Ah, I'll get that money to you soon, I promise."

Ouch. Okay, message received loud and clear. Reece nodded and simply got out of the car. He'd didn't even look back as he entered his building. *Well, that was fucking humiliating.*

Ben stared after him, well aware that he'd just done something wrong. *He just came onto me, didn't he? Despite acting like a fucking moron and destroying his bike, he was still interested. And you just...not only didn't get that, but... embarrassed him....*

"Aw, fuck!" He gripped the steering wheel tightly; his hands close together at the top of the wheel as he bent forward and leaned his forehead on them. *I deserve to be alone!*

He leaned back, looking at the building for a second before reaching to unbuckle his belt, but then he stopped. No, he wouldn't mess it up this time; there most certainly wouldn't be another chance so he would have to do this right. Putting on his signal, and looking very *carefully* around him, he pulled away. He'd find the nearest bike store. It was still mid-afternoon, there should be at least one somewhere that was still open.

Reece watched from his window as the police cruiser pulled away. He sighed and picked up his phone, dialing Darren's number.

"Darren, hi. Yeah, I'm fine, look, I need a favor."

BEN looked at all the different bikes without a clue where to start. He needed help. Stuffing his hands in his pockets, he craned his neck to see if there was any staff nearby.

"Are you all right there, sir?"

Ben looked around, and then down at a short, youngish woman who was wearing a badge that read, "My name is Stephanie, ask me for help."

"Help."

"I'm sorry?" She asked, frowning.

"Ahem." He shook his head minutely. "I could use some help. I'm looking for a bike."

Stephanie, who apparently had a sense of humor, looked pointedly at the racks and racks of bikes in front of them. "I think you came to the right place."

Ben offered a small smile. "I need a particular kind of bike. One that a bike messenger might use?"

She nodded. "Okay, I think we have a few in particular that seem popular for that purpose. Though to be honest most bike messengers tend to use just a standard mountain bike."

"I need a really good one though."

"Alright, boy or girl?"

"Huh?" *Real intelligent, Ben.*

"I'm assuming it's for someone else." She looked down at his uniform and then back up. "It'd be kind of difficult to attach the flashing lights and siren to one of these."

Ben laughed at the gentle teasing. "It's for a guy." He cleared his throat uncomfortably, and she tried to hide her smile. Ben rolled his eyes and couldn't help but grin. "Alright, here's how it is. I accidentally trashed the bike of this guy I know. A special guy...."

She seemed to understand, but simply pressed her lips in a tight line to keep from smiling and nodded her head. She was one professional bike sales person, Ben decided.

"I backed up over it and, well, it's in a dumpster now, and he's kind of screwed job-wise until he gets a new one."

"And it needs to be a really good one...." she trailed off, one brow lifting.

"You got it." Meaning: *Yes, lady, you have come to the correct conclusion. I need to impress this guy.*

"Okay, then, come with me."

Ben followed.

REECE refused to ride the fucking thing. He probably looked just as stupid walking it home, and he'd just have to ride it tomorrow, but for now he wouldn't even sit on it.

Fucking pink. With a basket, and a bell with a picture of a daisy on it. He knew he should be grateful to Darren for the loan, but he was presently in too foul a mood. His face must have been a picture:

"I assure you, buddy, whatever you can lend me will be just fi— what the fuck is that?"

"It's a bike, something you don't have right now."

"Well, if I ever doubted you were a fag before...."

"Fuck you, it belongs to Jenny."

"What are you doing with your sister's bike?"

"She left it here last time she visited. And call me the F word again and that bell is going up your ass. Then again, you might like that...."

"Darren, it's *pink*, for fuck's sake."

"Quit your bitching. It's got two wheels, it works, and it's free."

"When you put it like that…."

"That's what I thought."

"You sure Jenny won't mind?"

"Nah, she's always kind of had a thing for you."

"Gross. Jenny knows I'm gay."

"Like that'd matter to her. And I'll pretend you didn't just call my sister gross."

"You know that's not what I meant. I mean she… well, she dated my brother for God's sake."

A soft, sympathetic look had crossed Darren's face. "Yeah I know, I was kidding."

The conversation had fallen kind of flat after that, just like it usually did whenever he mentioned Ryan. He'd said thank you—sincerely this time—and left with the bike.

So now he was wheeling it back to his apartment. Luckily, it wasn't a long walk, and he'd only received a few odd glances. He stopped dead in his tracks, however, when he saw an all too familiar police car parked out front.

Reece groaned. Ben—make that Officer Jenkins—probably wanted to pay him back, and be free of the guilt so he could get out of there as soon as possible. He felt a little squeeze in his chest. He knew it wasn't Ben's fault, he couldn't help being straight, no one was perfect. But he'd gained a little crush since he'd seen him outside Roger's apartment, and, to be honest, he felt kind of stupid and embarrassed for thinking someone like that would go for him. Gay or straight.

Forcing himself to approach the side of the car, he bent to knock on the window, and then noticed that the car was empty. Great. He was likely upstairs, waiting outside his apartment. Did he even know which one was his? Would Reece have to invite him in for a drink to be friendly? Christ, that would be awkward. Letting himself in, he hefted the bike onto his shoulder and climbed the stairs. Nothing to it but to do it.

When he got to his floor he set the pink atrocity down, and was greeted by what he had to admit was a damned endearing sight.

Ben was there, sitting on the floor outside his door with his knees bent and his arms resting on them. He looked kind of nervous. Hearing Reece's approach his head shot up, and he gracefully got to his feet.

"Hi."

"Hello, Officer."

Ben seemed to deflate a little at the formal greeting. He cleared his throat and rubbed the back of his neck. "I um, wanted to apologize—"

Reece rolled his eyes and cut him off. "Seriously, apology accepted, don't worry about it...." Then he spotted the bike propped up behind Ben's large form.

"Actually I wanted to apologize for the way we parted a few hours ago. You kind of leapt out of the car before I could really get my thoughts in order and figure out what it was you were saying...."

Reece cleared his throat. Well, this was... he didn't know... romantic? He quickly stomped down the thought; no way was he putting himself out there again like that. Let Ben do the work.

"So, did you? Figure it out, I mean."

Ben gave him an utterly disarming smile. Really, the man was too gorgeous for his own good. "Well, I hope so. I was also hoping that you'd perhaps like to have dinner with me"—his voice became softer, perhaps a little unsure of himself—"some time, maybe...?" He petered off with a self-conscious shrug, lips lifted at one corner.

Reece allowed himself a small smile. How fucking cute was this man? But he wanted to be one hundred percent sure this was not guilt speaking for the guy. He nodded toward the bike behind him. "Tell me you didn't buy me that."

"I did." Ben stood aside so Reece could move closer and get a proper look.

"It's not as easy carrying a bike up those stairs as you make it look, you know," he joked. "I hope it's all right. The shop assistant was real helpful. She said it was better to get one that was slightly too small than too big, I tried to describe your height and build...."

"Oh, yeah?" Reece said, laughing. "What did you say?"

Ben grinned and stuffed his hands in his pockets. "Two or three inches shorter than I am, lean, trim body...." he looked Reece up and down as he said it.

Reece swallowed. "You never said that."

"I did, about your height anyway." He winked.

Reece couldn't really think of a damn thing to say. Ben shuffled his feet slightly and looked back at the bike. "I couldn't decide between a mountain bike with slick tires and a shorter wheelbase, or a road bike. She said the road bikes move a lot quicker and have more precise steering control, but that it wouldn't hold up as well as a mountain bike, or stop as quickly."

Reece just blinked at the guy.

Feeling uncomfortable, Ben continued. "Then there was a track bike. Moves quickly, has fewer components so the upkeep would be cheaper, and is supposedly fun to ride. But apparently the least comfortable? So...."

"So you went with a mountain bike. The most expensive one you could apparently find."

"Well, it's supposed to be the easiest to handle in traffic, and the safest. I figured that was the most important thing."

"Ben... you really didn't have to do this." He was beyond touched.

Witness

Ben seemed a bit disappointed by his words, and shrugged. "I kept the receipt, if you don't like it...."

"Are you kidding?" Reece laughed. "Have you seen my alternative?" He pointed to the pink bike.

Ben smiled, though it seemed a little forced. "Well, it's yours, anyway." He touched the back of his head in that nervous gesture, and spoke in a tone that was just a little overly bright. "So I guess that's a no to dinner, huh?" He smiled that crooked smile.

Reece blinked; no, it definitely was not a no to dinner.

Ben waved his hand dismissively. "Don't worry about it, I totally understand." He swallowed. "I think I might take off...."

"Wait!" Reece blurted, stepping closer and holding up a hand to stop him. "I'd love—" he stopped and laughed a little at the over-eagerness in his voice. "I mean, I'd like that. Dinner, with you."

Ben's smile was slow and warm. "Yeah?"

"Yes. Though, I just want to make sure"—he licked his bottom lip briefly and stepped right up to Ben—"is this dinner to make up for today? Because... seriously, the bike more than does that, trust me."

Ben frowned, and then gave him that crooked smile again. Reece's breath caught—actually caught right there in his throat—when Ben's fingers brushed just under his chin, his thumb gently touching the underside of Reece's bottom lip.

"No. It wouldn't be to make up for anything. It would be because I haven't been able to stop thinking about you since the first time I saw you. It'd be because I want to know you."

Reece refused to swoon just on principle. Men didn't fucking swoon, even the gay ones. But he did take a deep breath and let it out quickly with a smile.

"Thank God. You have no idea how frustrated I was getting trying to figure out what team you play for."

Ben dropped his hand and laughed. "Yours."

"Well, go me."

"So." Ben tilted his head, grinning, "Are you free this weekend?"

"I believe I am."

"You mentioned you didn't drive?"

"That's right." Reece answered quickly. It wasn't exactly his favorite topic of conversation.

"So I can pick you up? Say Saturday, eight o'clock?"

"Sounds good to me. I look forward to it."

"I'll make a reservation. Anything you don't like?"

"I pretty much like all food." Reece said, laughing. God, he must be grinning like an idiot. He was being "picked up," though he knew logically he couldn't very well ride his awesome new bike there—helmet hair wasn't sexy—it still made him feel a little giddy.

"Can I get your number in the meantime? Just in case." Ben pulled a small note book and pen out of his jacket as he spoke.

"Oh, I think you got my number," Reece said with a wicked grin, then reeled off his actual number, feeling happier than he had in a long time.

Putting the note pad away, Ben stepped up closer, looked into Reece's eyes and spoke softly, almost seductively. "I'll see you real soon, Reece."

"I look forward to it," he repeated, unsure if he was about to be kissed.

Then Ben was walking past him, smiling over his shoulder until he reached the stairs. He gave a quick wave, and then was gone. Reece let out the breath he'd been unconsciously holding.

"Ah, shit," he said, laughing..

He was swooning, just ever so slightly.

Chapter 4

It had been a long time since Ben had to get ready for a date. He'd decided on black jeans, polished boots, and a light blue button-down shirt. He took a deep breath and blew it out slowly as he regarded his reflection. He looked good, he supposed. The shirt pulled across his biceps if he bent his elbow too far—maybe he should subtract a few pounds off the weights?—but that would be okay as long as he didn't flex. And seeing as he wasn't a show-off asshole, that shouldn't be a problem.

He did, however, wish that he'd checked his wardrobe to see if his "going out" clothes still fit him all right. As well as the shirt stretching a tiny bit over his upper arms and chest when he moved, he'd lost about an inch off his waist. Luckily this was easily resolved with a belt. He deliberated on changing the shirt, then decided against it. Sharon had once commented that it brought out his eyes. And while he couldn't really see what she was going on about, he'd take anything he could get that worked in his favor tonight.

His hair could have done with a cut; it was by no means long, just not as short as he usually kept it. He touched it up a little with some gel, just to keep it in order, and decided that he actually didn't look half bad.

"Well, Mud, how'd I look?"

His cat lay curled up fast asleep on his pillow. She didn't so much as stir.

"Yeah, thanks."

Going downstairs, he did a mental check list. Aftershave? Check. Wallet? He patted his back pocket: check. Keys? Check. He'd even given his truck a wash. Now all he needed to do was pick what jacket to wear. He had a nice black suit jacket he could wear, or his leather jacket. He figured that Reece had only ever actually seen him in uniform, so he decided to go with the leather. It was black and nicely worn in without looking banged up. It was also his favorite jacket, and he wasn't going on this date tonight as Officer Ben Jenkins. Tonight he was just Ben.

He checked his watch, then locked up the house and made his way to his truck. He felt nervous, but it was a good nervous.

REECE stood before his wardrobe wearing shoes, dark blue jeans, and nothing else. He went to run his hands through his hair and managed to stop himself; he'd just got it reasonably tame and didn't want to ruin it. It wasn't easy for him to pull off the tousled-yet-tidy look; usually, his hair decided to just go whichever way it chose.

He couldn't decide which shirt to wear. He figured he stood a chance at looking okay whatever he wore, seeing as Ben had only ever seen him in his cycling gear. Still, he wanted to make the effort, if not to impress, then to boost his confidence. His bed was already covered in the items he'd rejected, and he was running out of choices. It had been a while since he'd treated himself to some new clothes, figuring that food and electricity were more important.

Taking out a thin dark gray sweater, he pulled it on and checked in the mirror. Not bad. Darren had always liked this one on him. Though he didn't really want to think of Darren or the last conversation he'd had with him at that precise moment. He'd been kind of pissed at him for killing his buzz. He hadn't meant to, and he knew his buddy was just looking out for him, as usual, but he was a big boy, and Ben already seemed so much different from the last guy he'd dated.

"Just keep a little bit of yourself back this time, you know?"

"What the hell does that mean?"

"Don't get all pissed, all I meant… just let it develop, yeah? He sounds like a real nice guy and everything; I mean, I can't believe he actually bought you a new bike! Even if he did trash your old one—"

"Yeah, well that's the kind of guy he is."

"See, you're sounding besotted already. You're my best friend, Reece, and I'm not saying you will be, but I don't want to see you hurt again. Not like the last time, the last guy."

"That was my own fault, I can see that now. It was obvious to everyone but me that we would never get past the fucking stage, I just wanted it to."

"You get why, don't you?"

"Yes. I know."

"I don't know why you get so down on yourself sometimes. You're cute; you're funny and so talented."

"Stop sucking up. Still pissed here."

"For once I'm not kidding. You tried to force your last relationship into something more than it could ever be, all because of this weird hang-up of yours. You just gotta relax once in a while and let the chips fall where they may, you know?"

Reece had sighed. He knew Darren was right, but didn't want to admit it. "I guess."

"You have no idea how much respect I have for you, Reece. I mean that. Will you promise me something? Please?"

"I guess I owe you that much. Shoot."

"Just be yourself with this guy. Let whatever happens, happen. In its own time."

"I can do that." He'd gripped the receiver a little tighter. "Okay, I'll do that."

"Love you, Reece. This guy sounds special. Don't let this conversation mess with you, and have an awesome time."

"Yeah, I'll do that. Love you too."

"Call me after or something, we can dissect, and you can gush if you like."

"I don't gush."

Darren laughed. "Talk soon,"

"Soon."

And he wouldn't let the conversation mess with him. But he would take Darren's advice to heart, even if it annoyed him to do so.

The sweater fit him perfectly and was made of really soft material. The little V neck suited him, seeming to elongate him a bit. Nodding in satisfaction, he fastened his watch and nearly jumped out of his skin at the sound of his buzzer.

Shit. He smiled at his own nervousness and pressed the button to speak.

"Hello?"

"Hi, Reece, it's Ben."

"Hey, Ben, come on up. I'm almost ready."

He buzzed Ben in, and waited by the door until he heard the knock. It took Ben a little while to get there. Opening up, he couldn't help the warm smile that spread across his lips when he saw Ben again.

"Hey, get lost?"

"No, I ran into Roger."

"Say no more," Reece said. He could only guess at how Ben managed to avoid being roped into a game of cards by the loveable old guy.

"Come on in. I just need to grab a jacket. I apologize for the mess."

He had, in fact, cleaned his apartment from head to toe that day, just in case the date turned into a sleepover. But it seemed the polite thing to say.

"What mess?" Ben asked, laughing.

Reece smiled in reply, reaching in the closet for his jacket.

"You look real nice, Reece."

The words were spoken so softly that Reece actually felt a little heat touch his cheeks. It didn't seem right that a man could be so hot and adorable at the same time.

"Thank you. You look goddamn edible." Had he not just fucking said that?

Ben laughed in surprise. "Well, thanks."

Reece paused in slipping one arm into his jacket when realizing what he'd said. "I can't believe I just said that," he said with a laugh, "and here I was planning on being all charming and shit."

Ben laughed again and then moved behind him to help him with the jacket, sliding his hands over Reece's shoulders after. The simple action seemed gentlemanly.

"It was charming, in your own way."

Reece turned to face Ben, adjusting the collar. "In my way, huh? What way is that?"

Ben tilted his head in mock thought. "Cute and sexy as hell?"

"Cute and sexy I can live with."

Ben grinned. "Shall we go?"

They headed down to the street, and Reece laughed when he caught himself looking for the cruiser. "For some reason I expected to see your cop car."

Ben smiled. "Well, it certainly would have gotten us to the restaurant quicker, especially if I gave the siren and lights a whirl. But I figured you wouldn't want the attention."

"You figured right. Nice truck."

"Thanks. So how come you never got your license?"

Reece ignored the weight that settled in his stomach, the same weight that appeared every time he was asked that question.

"Oh, you know," he drawled, "a bike's so much more environmentally friendly and all that. Not to mention that I'm not exactly a fan of exercise, and seeing as my day and any travel involves riding a bike for the most part, I don't have to worry about vegetating in my down time."

"Huh, that makes sense I guess."

"You sound surprised."

"Well," Ben shrugged, indicating to take the next left, "the few times I've seen you you've been in those tight-fitted cycling clothes." He looked over at Reece and grinned. "Which I find hot by the way." He smiled when Reece laughed.

"And you, well—" Ben wondered if he was being too forward. "You seem to be pretty fit." He shrugged, wondering if that just sounded like he was trying to stroke Reece's ego. He hoped not.

"Wow, you're good for my confidence." Reece laughed, and to be honest he suddenly felt pretty good about himself. Until then he hadn't been sure if he really measured up to this good-looking guy.

"I'm not just saying that or anything but, yeah. I guess I see how the bike makes sense. Hell, if I did the same I wouldn't have to work out as much as I do."

"Might take you longer to catch bad guys, though."

Ben laughed. "It might make taking them in a bit difficult, yeah."

"I don't know, you could cuff them to the handle bars? Sit them in a basket?"

"That prospect might just be enough to convince them not to commit the crime in the first place."

"Well if you need a bike, let me know, I got this real pretty pink one sitting at home...."

Ben laughed. "Where the hell did you get that anyway?"

"Borrowed it off my friend Darren," Reece continued with a chuckle when he saw the look Ben shot him. "It's his sister's, not his. I was desperate, remember? This really gorgeous cop had just totaled my ten-speed."

Ben shook his head. "What a jerk."

"Nah, he's alright."

Ben smiled warmly at him as he pulled up outside the restaurant. He was having a good time already. "Here we are."

"Great, let's go stuff our faces."

Ben smiled. "Sounds good to me."

"How's your food?" Ben asked.

"Unbelievable."

Speaking of unbelievable, Reece couldn't take his eyes away from Ben. The guy was wearing a shirt the same shade as his gorgeous baby blues that stretched slightly over his chest and arms. This was the first time Reece had gotten a real look at Ben, and the guy was fucking ripped. He was suddenly glad that Ben hadn't taken his jacket off at his apartment; he probably would have jumped the guy.

"I adore food," he said around a mouth of steak, careful not to spit and gesturing to his plate with his fork. "I don't think there's any food I *don't* like."

"I know exactly what you mean. There's so many different tastes and textures to play with. I love how a home-cooked meal can just warm you through or have sentimental value, you know? Spicy, sweet, savory or a sticky, gooey dessert...." Ben trailed off "What, what's that look?"

"Nothing," Reece said, laughing gently, looking down at his steak as he cut it before grinning back at Ben wickedly. "I've just never found someone talking about food a turn-on before."

Ben coughed a little, bringing his napkin to his lips as his cheeks took on a slightly rosy hue. Reece laughed, finding the man's reaction rather endearing.

"You're one of those guys who gets bashful when complimented, aren't you?"

"I wouldn't say bashful." Ben protested.

"Aw, man, I don't stand a chance with you."

Ben frowned slightly. "What do you mean?"

Reece leaned across the table a little and spoke quietly. "You're fun, kind of sweet, and you look like you could bench press this table, with me sitting on it."

Ben smiled crookedly as he looked down at his plate, unsure what to say.

"You see?" Reece sat back. "You're freakin' cute too. Think I might have hit the jackpot when you ran over my bike."

"No, that'd be me."

Reece smiled. "So you got a passion for food, then, huh?"

"That's a bit of an understatement. If I hadn't been a cop I'd probably have wanted to train to be a chef."

"Oooh, you cook?"

"I like to, yeah." Ben gave him a handsome grin. "Maybe you could come over and I'll cook for you some time?"

Reece beamed. "Yeah I'd like that."

"Great, I'll think of something special."

"You're going to spoil me, aren't you?"

"Probably won't be able to help myself. To be honest, if I didn't work out I'd probably weight about five hundred pounds by now."

Reece laughed. "Exercise nut, huh?"

"I like lifting weights."

"I can tell," Reece said in a low voice, gazing hungrily at the man's torso.

Ben grinned. Usually he might not think anything of the attention, but coming from this man, it made him feel damn good. "And running. I've been known to get up at five a.m. to run a couple of miles before work."

Reece's eyes widened. "Five a.m.? There's a five a.m.?"

Ben laughed. "Not an early riser?"

"If you only knew the issues I have with getting up on time. Though that's not entirely my fault; I have a rather schizophrenic alarm clock."

Ben laughed louder than he meant to and put his fork down to cover his mouth with his napkin. Reece just beamed.

"You have a great laugh."

"Well, you seem to have a way of putting things that tickle me."

Reece just grinned. Had he ever had so much fun on a date? "So why didn't you?"

"Why didn't I what?"

"Become a chef instead of a cop?"

"Oh, I see. Well, I wanted to be a cop more, I guess. My dad was one, and I admired him so much that it just felt the natural thing to do."

"Is he…?" Reece couldn't help but pick up on the past tense.

"Yeah, about three years ago. I moved out when I went to college, then applied to the academy. My ex-partner was actually my dad's last partner."

"Oh really? That's so cool." Reece smiled.

"Yeah, he got injured a couple months back, though. He's retiring early."

"Nothing too serious, I hope?"

"No, he's got a limp that probably won't go away, but he's nearly fifty and has a wife and twin girls to think about."

Reece made an agreeing noise, nodding, encouraging him to continue.

"So I moved back three years ago into the house I grew up in. It was always just me and dad rambling about in that house—I never knew my mom, she passed away shortly after I was born, but despite it only ever having been the two of us, the place seems so much bigger now that he's not there."

"I bet. Did you ever think of selling it?" Reece asked gently, tilting his head slightly, "or too many memories?"

"I did think about it, but couldn't quite bring myself to do it. It's the last little bit of him, you know?" He shrugged.

"I'm sorry, that must be difficult. I imagine you guys must have been really close." Reece moved his hand across the table to touch Ben's.

Ben smiled, warmed by the gesture, and let his fingers brush over Reece's. "Sometimes, but I've got some good friends. Friends are just the family we choose, aren't they?"

Reece squeezed his hand. "You got that right."

Ben's thumb rubbed over Reece's knuckle. "So how long have you been a bike messenger? You like it?"

"I've been doing it nearly ten years now, about the same time I've lived at my apartment."

"What was that little grimace about?" Ben asked him.

"You noticed that, huh?" He laughed. "Well, I'm actually a freelance photographer. I even have an ad in the local papers: Reece's Family Portraits."

"No kidding." Ben seemed impressed by that, so Reece continued.

"Yeah, I landed in this neck of the woods when I was nineteen. Darren, my friend I mentioned? He's actually my best friend, my oldest pal. He owns his own business now, the one I work for. Back then, before he owned it, he managed to get me a job by talking to his boss. So I got the job, and now Darren owns the place, which is handy considering how late I always am." He laughed.

"He sounds like a good guy."

"He's the best. The job helped me through college, with a little help from my parents, of course, and it pays the bills now but...."

"But you'd rather be doing your photography."

"You got it right on the nose. I'm one of those struggling artists, but far less pretentious."

Ben laughed.

A waiter came by to take their plates. Their hands parted with a quick squeeze, and they were offered the dessert menu.

"You want one?" Ben asked.

"How about we split one?" Reece asked. He looked at the waiter. "Can we get the chocolate cake slice with a vanilla scoop, two spoons?"

Ben liked it—Reece feeling comfortable enough to order for them like that, just two spoons over a shared dessert.

"Is that okay?"

"It's good."

Dessert arrived promptly and Reece made yummy noises—unable to help himself and making Ben laugh. They both leaned forward on their elbows, their heads close together as they dug in.

"So good," Reece moaned.

"So if I ever need to bribe you in the future, all I need is chocolate cake?"

Reece snorted. "You batting those pretty eyes of yours would probably do the trick."

Ben grinned, red creeping up his neck again, and Reece groaned again. "See? Cute."

They dug in, and both chuckled quietly as their spoons battled playfully, like hockey sticks, for the gooey part. "Get back on your side of the plate," Reece said, chuckling low in his throat. Looking up at Ben, their heads so close, he couldn't help but glance down at the man's lips.

"Tell you what," Ben murmured, "I'll swap you the last bite for a kiss."

Reece smiled widely and then nodded. "That sounds like one hell of a deal." He laughed quietly as Ben held up the last bite to his lips on his spoon. They were sitting toward the outskirts of the restaurant so they had privacy, but in that moment it honestly felt as if they were the only ones there.

Ben laughed as chocolate sauce smeared a little over Reece's chin. He brushed it away with his thumb and then licked his thumb clean. Reece's big brown eyes just sparkled at him. He nodded his head a little, the universal sign for "come here." Reece leaned in, swallowing his last bite and grinning impishly.

It wasn't deep or passionate, but it was a perfect first kiss. They both smiled into it, lips gently brushing, tasting of chocolate and vanilla. Reece began to pull away and then laughed quietly when Ben's lips followed his, prolonging the kiss.

"Even better than the dessert," Reece flirted.

A waiter appeared at that point, his lips pressed together, obviously trying to smother a grin.

"Will that be all, sirs?"

Ben looked to Reece, who nodded.

"Yes, thank you, just the bill."

CLIMBING out of Ben's truck, Reece took a steadying breath, his previous conversation with Darren running through his mind. It would be very easy to invite Ben in, but he also wanted to just let whatever had sparked up between them take its natural course. This attraction was too good to screw up.

Ben came to stand beside him outside the building door, smiling almost knowingly as he moved close, his hands shoved into his pockets.

"You're debating over whether to invite me in, aren't you?" He asked with a grin.

That surprised a laugh out of Reece. "Actually, yes. I'd love to invite you in"—he stepped closer—"and have you stay. But I'm kind of eager to get that second date you spoke about, and I don't want to screw this up. I realize of course that now I sound like a girl...."

Ben laughed and shook his head. One hand came out of his pocket to gently touch Reece's cheek. "How about," he said softly, "I kiss you goodnight now. Then I come pick you up Tuesday evening and cook for you?"

"Yeah? You don't mind?"

Ben shook his head. "I don't have to be into work the day after until the afternoon." He bit his lip briefly. "Think you could swing Wednesday morning off of work?"

Reece took a deep breath, knowing what Ben was asking. "That won't be a problem."

"Good," Ben murmured, and leaned down that short distance to close the gap between them.

Reece smiled into the kiss. He opened his lips slightly, their tongues touching hesitantly at first, and then with more passion. Ben groaned, his hand pulling Reece close by the nape of his neck. Reece's hands clutched at Ben's jacket, then wound their way around his waist, clutching him close as his head was tilted back ever so slightly.

When they pulled away, their brows touched together for a moment, their breathing slightly labored.

"I've had the best time tonight. Thank you," Reece murmured.

"Thank you." Ben pressed their lips together again, softly this time. "I'll call you about Tuesday, okay?"

"Yeah." Reece nodded and let Ben pull away, almost regretfully.

He smiled warmly, held his hand up when Ben waved before pulling away, and then headed inside. He was tempted to call Darren to tell him all about it but decided that he wanted to keep this afterglow to himself for a bit. Besides, he was afraid he might gush.

CHAPTER 5

"So WHEN you said big...." Reece leaned forward against his seatbelt, looking through the windshield. Despite the darkness, he could easily see the large house coming into view. It was lovely, two floors with a porch and a large yard. "You meant—"

"Big, yes."

"It must have been great growing up here."

"Oh yeah. You see those yellow rose bushes? They're not budding right now, but my mother planted those, and around the back there's a twenty-six-year-old fort."

"You had a fort?" The idea of Ben playing in a fort as a kid made Reece grin.

Ben nodded. "My dad made it. It's like a tree house, but not very high off the ground. He was always terrified that I'd fall or hurt myself."

"I guess after losing your mother...." Reece said softly.

"Yeah, he was always protective of me."

"That's nice." Reece smiled. "I'm glad you had that."

"Are you close to your folks?"

Reece lifted his shoulder in a shrug. "I don't see them as often as I should, but I guess you could say I have a good relationship with them."

"I'm sure they adore you. You're kind of cute, ya know?"

"Flatterer." Reece reached over and gently shoved Ben's shoulder.

"Here we are," Ben said. He unbuckled and climbed out of the truck. Reece followed. "So, you got any brothers or sisters?" Ben asked, holding his hand out.

"No, no siblings." Reece slid his own loosely into it and allowed Ben to guide him up the few steps to the porch. He was glad Ben had his back to him when he dropped his hand to unlock the door. Reece looked up at the house, and a grin split his lips. "Who's that?"

"Hmm? Oh, that's Mud."

"Mud?"

Ben led them inside, shimmied his jacket off, and then helped Reece with his. "Go say hello if you like."

Reece wandered into a very comfortable-looking living room and went over to the window where a very odd-looking cat sat staring at him, its tail twitching.

"Hey, beautiful. Well, ain't you the cutest little fluff ball I've ever seen." He stroked the scruffy cat, smiling as a little head pushed its way into his hand. "Why 'Mud'?"

"Short for Muddles."

Reece laughed. "Fitting. I have a fish called Wesley Snipes."

Ben's laugh startled him a little; he hadn't realized the man was standing behind him. He turned, and went willingly as Ben pulled him close with a gentle tug at his waist.

"I've wanted to kiss you since you got into my truck," Ben murmured.

Reece's hands bunched gently at the front of Ben's T-shirt so he could pull him down for a kiss. Ben groaned and gently cupped the back of Reece's head while pulling him against his body.

Witness

Ben slid his lips along Reece's neck as his hand moved from the man's trim waist to cup his rear and squeeze gently. He heard Reece sigh softly and then suddenly go still. His hands stopped what they were doing. "Something wrong?"

Reece pulled his head back a fraction to look Ben in the eye. "Can I smell lasagna? You're cooking lasagna?"

Ben rolled his eyes and grinned.

"I fucking *love* lasagna."

Ben snorted and tugged him into a brief hug before pulling away and leading him to the kitchen. "Has anyone ever told you that your potty mouth is kind of a turn-on?"

"You should hear me when I'm getting laid," Reece teased, winking.

Ben grinned back wickedly. "Careful, I'll take that as a challenge."

"Hope so. Just feed me first."

Ben shook his head. "Christ, you crack me up."

Ben put on a mitt and bent to open the oven. He pulled out the dish and took a look at the lasagna. "This should be done in a few more minutes."

As soon as the door opened, that fantastic smell hit Reece for real. It looked so good. He couldn't help the groan that left his lips, and grinned sheepishly when his stomach growled.

"You and food!" Ben laughed, putting the dish back into the oven and closing the door. "Did you eat at all today?"

"Hey, you're talking to a man who lives on microwave meals, cereal, and Pop-Tarts. I can't cook for shit so it doesn't get much better than this for me. And I had a pretzel this morning; I've been leaving space for the cooking you boasted about."

"Good. Oh, and it does get better." Ben's smirk was very promising.

"Don't tease me, man, not when it comes to my stomach."

"How's homemade bread with fresh salad as a starter, and then blueberry pie made with berries picked from my back yard for dessert sound?"

Reece blinked. "God. You're like Martha Stewart. But fuckable and with handcuffs."

The laugh that ripped from Ben made Reece grin. He couldn't help but want the man near, so he hooked his fingertips into the waistband of Ben's jeans and pulled him close, loosely wrapping his arms around Ben's waist. His lips brushed the still chortling man's jaw.

"Stop laughing already and feed me!"

Ben's laugh was infectious.

"You don't even need to give me a plate. I'll eat it right out of the dish with a spoon. Feed me, man."

That just started the laughter up again, so Reece decided that there was only one way to stop it. He reached up with both hands and pulled Ben down for a kiss. It seemed to do the trick. Ben gave a surprised moan, and the kiss deepened instantly.

Reece breathed heavily out of his nose, moaning as he threaded his fingers tightly through Ben's hair. Ben growled and then walked them clumsily back against the counter, his large hands moving down Reece's back.

"God, Ben." The sudden heat between them shocked Reece.

Ben moved his hands underneath Reece's thighs and lifted him onto the counter as if he didn't weigh anything. He inserted himself between Reece's thighs and wrapped those strong legs around his waist.

"Jesus," Reece gasped before his mouth was taken again roughly. His hands began to wander desperately. Ben was just so gorgeous, so big; he wanted to touch him everywhere at once. He laid his hands on those broad shoulders and then let them slide down to grip firm biceps.

His hand skimmed down between them, past what he was sure was a six-pack under that shirt, to cup greedily at the bulge in the cop's jeans. Ben hissed.

"You are so fucking sexy," Reece ground out, teeth clenched as Ben attacked his neck. He pulled Ben's head back, needing that mouth back on his. Reece pawed at Ben's T-shirt, tugging it up. Their lips parted for a second so that he could pull it over Ben's head, just as an egg timer buzzed, signaling that the food was ready.

They both paused, glancing at the oven. Ben looked back to him, his brow raised in question. Reece worried his lip. He was starving and it smelled so good. Like Ben, he glanced from the oven to his kissing partner, and they both grinned.

"We have all evening." Ben murmured.

Reece let go of the man's T-shirt and watched with hungry eyes as Ben adjusted himself; he wasn't faring much better. Ben gently stroked the tousled brown hair off of Reece's brow, and kissed him.

"Hmm." Reece followed Ben's lips when the man pulled away, making him grin.

"Thought you wanted feeding?"

"I do but... you're all—and that smells so good. Oh, God, I've short circuited."

Ben smiled, turned Reece in the direction of the dining table, and patted him on the ass.

"I'll still be here later, but lasagna is best eaten hot. Go, sit, I'll bring the food over."

"Sure I can't help?"

"Here, take the salad and bread."

Reece took the starters to the table, then came back. "Cutlery?" He pulled open a drawer in a search for some.

"Next one over. You want anything in particular to drink? I've got wine, beer, water?"

"Water's fine for me, thanks."

"Go sit your ass down."

Reece grinned and sat down, happy to watch as Ben brought over two plates of food, putting one down in front of Reece, then the other opposite him. He liked that it was a small table in the spacious room; it felt more intimate. He watched as Ben went to the fridge to uncap a bottle of water and pour it into two glasses.

"It's killing you waiting, isn't it?" Ben teased.

"I'm sitting on my hands. Answer your question?"

"It's okay, dig in." Ben reached for the wall and the light in the room dimmed. Finally he sat down opposite Reece.

"You know, I used to want a dimmer in my apartment. I've always thought they were classy and romantic. But it just seemed silly to put one in my place, like dressing up a hippopotamus by putting diamond earrings on it or something."

Ben snorted and nearly dropped his fork. "I'm afraid to eat in case you make me choke."

"I'll be good." Reece took a piece of homemade bread and mopped up some of the sauce. It tasted amazing. "You know, you're going to make a great housewife some day."

Ben shook his head, his shoulders beginning to move up and down as he quickly swallowed what he was eating. Reece held up his hands in apology. "Sorry," he said, and laughed.

The lasagna was delicious. He attempted to say as much around a mouthful, making Ben grin and wink at him.

"I think you missed your calling. I mean I know you're probably a great cop, and I'm pretty sure you've given me a uniform fetish, but this is some decent chow, Ben."

Ben quirked an eyebrow. "Uniform fetish?"

"Oh, yeah, big time. I've never found an authority figure a turn-on before, but you make it look good." He grinned deviously for a moment and then tried to sound as sexy as possible, but ended up laughing through his words: "You can arrest me anytime."

"Oh good Lord." Ben lowered his knife and fork, shaking his head again.

"I'm so sorry," Reece said, chuckling, "that was tacky, even for me."

"I don't know about tacky, tempting maybe...."

"Then I reiterate my offer!"

"I think I like the idea of coming home to you cuffed up, though you'd need to break the law first."

"I'll make sure to jaywalk at the very next opportunity."

Ben smiled brightly. "Just be careful, I don't want you hurt."

Reece put down his knife and fork. "It's no good. C'mere."

"Why?" Ben laughed.

"Just do it, c'mere and kiss me. Now."

"Bossy little thing," Ben muttered before leaning across the table to kiss him.

Reece hummed happily into the kiss. "You're really good at that," he sighed when Ben sat back down.

"Kissing?"

"Kissing me."

"Not exactly a hardship." Ben gave him a heated look. "So you got tomorrow off of work okay?" He'd felt the tingle of anticipation when he'd picked Reece up and saw him swing a backpack into the backseat of his truck.

Reece grinned mischievously. "Yeah, Darren was fine. I just had to tell him you were cooking for me, and he tried to give me the entire week off."

"I think I like this guy."

"Well, he thinks you're too good to be true ever since I showed up to work with the new bike. He's a hopeless romantic."

"I wouldn't say running over your old one was romantic."

"No. But debating with a sales person over which one to buy me, then sitting outside my apartment with it until I got home was. Made me melt a little, anyway."

The look Ben gave him was decidedly intimate.

"So, your house is amazing," Reece said. "What I've seen of it, that is."

"I can give you the five-cent tour after we're done here, if you like."

Reece shook his head. "We've got plenty of time. So, you always lived here with your dad? Before college, I mean."

"Yeah. Houses were cheaper in this area in the early seventies. It wasn't in great shape when he bought it, but he was very good with his hands; he fixed it up at minimal cost. He and my mom married young and wanted a whole gaggle of kids. He told me that she would save every penny they made so that it could be poured into their dream home to raise them. It's worth a fortune now, but...."

"But there's a history. A lot of love went into this house. I can understand why you wouldn't want to let it go."

Ben shrugged. "It's not as full of life as they'd planned for it, but I try to keep it in decent shape. I take care of the garden, upkeep, things like that. It'd feel disrespectful to them not to."

"You're a good son."

"I hope so."

Reece smiled brightly. "I bet your dad was so proud of you when you joined the force."

Ben grinned. "At the ceremony he was there with all his cop friends, introducing me as Officer Jenkins."

Witness

"A *real* proud father, then." Reece laughed.

"He took so many pictures of me when I first got my uniform. Then again, he was always taking pictures of me. For a family of just two, he managed to fill several photo albums."

"I would so love to see pictures of you as a kid. I bet you were an adorable little guy, and a really handsome teenager. Girls all over you—if only they knew."

"I was a super-quiet, shy kid. And try awkward and lanky as a teenager. The muscle didn't come along till my mid-twenties," Ben said.

Reece tilted his head. "Aw, man, now I *have* to see the pictures. Pictures are my job, remember?"

"They're not exactly up to a professional's standards."

"I love pictures taken by family. It's so great to see the bond between the person in the picture and the person taking it. They're the best kind."

"Sentimental." Ben accused playfully. "Is that why you chose portraits? Reece's Family Portraits. I may have looked for the ad."

"Why?" Reece laughed.

Ben shrugged. "Just curious. So is it?"

"Not exactly. While it's still photography, family portraits are just another way to pay the bills while doing something that resembles my chosen field."

"What would you rather be taking pictures of?"

Reece took a deep breath and smiled a little self consciously. "There's no one thing really. Family portraits are okay, but can be a little stale, you know?"

"How do you mean?"

"Well, they can be a little false. These families get dressed up, and can seem so uncomfortable with their plastered-on smiles. Again, it pays the bills but I prefer something more genuine, a shot taken in the moment, nothing forced. That's why I love old family photo albums—you mostly always see a genuine reaction. Whether it's a picture of an excited kid opening Christmas presents, or a birthday party or a picnic—the best pictures are always the ones where the individual in focus has no idea their picture is being taken. Their expression is completely open and whatever their emotions—they're just lying there, bare, because they don't know to hide it. You're witnessing a small part of who they are without them knowing it."

"Wow," Ben murmured.

"Saying that," Reece said, placing his knife and fork down on his now clean plate—Christ he'd eaten that fast, "I adore landscape photos. I don't get to travel as much as I'd like to—to boost my portfolio—but some of the best shots can be found in your own back yard, so to speak."

"Where would you go, if you could go anywhere?" Ben asked.

"It might sound odd, but I'd love to go to Iceland."

"Iceland?" Ben laughed.

"Not great for sunbathing, I know," Reece said, grinning. "But, God, what I'd give to see the Northern lights. I've only ever seen images taken by other photographers, but they're heartbreakingly beautiful, Ben. Nature at its most spectacular."

Ben smiled almost wistfully, He had a feeling Reece could make anything sound beautiful. "So, you have a portfolio?"

"Yeah, sure I do. Quite a few, actually. I've got more than ten years' work accumulated now."

"I'd love to see your work sometime."

"Sure, though they're not all good. Sure as hell can't seem to sell them," Reece said.

"So you try to sell those kinds of pictures as well? To who?"

Witness

"Magazines, publishers—you know, for book covers. Art stores, galleries. Anyone, really."

"You're an artist. I don't know why I never thought of it that way before."

"That's because I'm not, I'm a bike messenger slash wannabe artist." Reece kidded, though it did hit a nerve.

"No way, you sound so passionate when you talk about it. You light right up."

"I do?" Reece flushed slightly.

"Yeah, it's pretty amazing."

Reece laughed a little self-consciously. "Okay, you get to see the photos."

Ben smiled, and nodded at Reece's plate. "Are you done, or would you like seconds?"

"As wonderful as it was, Chef, I should probably leave room for dessert."

"Good idea."

"It was delicious, Ben, thank you."

"No problem, why don't you head on into the living room and make yourself comfortable? We'll have dessert a little later or something."

"Let me help you with the dishes first."

Ben waved a hand. "Go on through. I have a huge DVD collection. Go pick something boring so we can ignore it and make out."

Reece laughed and went into the living room. There were indeed a lot of DVDs to choose from. "Oh, hey," he said, speaking up so Ben would hear him in the kitchen "You're a Hitchcock fan? I love old films!"

"Yeah? I'm a big Jimmy Stewart fan myself."

"Love him. There's something so likeable about him, isn't there?"

Reece pulled out *Rear Window*—awesome film. "I'm gonna pretend to be scared so I can cuddle up close, just so you know."

Ben came back carrying two glasses of wine. He handed one to Reece, and Reece handed him the DVD he'd chosen. "Cutie, you could put *The Lion King* on and cuddle up to me if you like. I really don't mind."

Reece raised an eyebrow. "Cutie?"

Ben blinked in surprise and then smiled apologetically. "Sorry, didn't realize I'd said that out loud."

"That's fine by me, handsome." Reece gave him a quick kiss and then walked over to the couch. He paused by the fireplace where a series of framed photos sat on the mantel.

"Oh, hey," he said softly, "is this your dad?"

The photo was obviously a little dated, but the resemblance was undeniable. A serious but kind face stared out of the picture. The man was in uniform, his shoulders held high and straight. Blue eyes—a slightly different shade than Ben's, black hair and a strong jaw. Though Ben's handsome features were less severe, he was very nearly the spitting image of his father.

"Yeah, that's him."

"Your hero, huh?"

Ben shrugged and smiled. "Yeah. I'm who I am today because of him. He made sure I had a happy childhood, taught me everything. How to ride a bike, how to shave, how to drive, how to treat other people. He even taught me how to cook and garden. You know, some of my best memories are of the two of us when he'd take me fishing. Just me and him, out by some quiet lake. He was amazing when I figured out I was gay."

"Oh, yeah? He didn't mind?"

Witness

Ben laughed. "I'm sure he knew before I did. I don't think he minded because he was a very open-minded guy—for a cop. To be honest, I don't think he'd let anything come between us. Perhaps if my mother had been around it might not have seemed so insignificant, I'm not sure. He just made it clear that if I was, it wouldn't be wrong, that he'd love me no differently, and that he'd always be there for me."

"Wow."

"Yeah. I got lucky with a parent like that. I miss him."

"I can tell." Reece stroked Ben's arm. "And is that your mom?"

Another frame held a photo of Ben's father with his arm around the waist of a beautiful young woman. She had dark brown curls, a lovely smile, and the exact same blue eyes as Ben. *There you are. A perfect mishmash of two beautiful people.*

"Yep, I wish I'd known her."

"You have her eyes."

"Apparently so, yeah."

Reece studied the images for a moment. "He seems like the kind of guy you'd want to be friends with, you know?"

Ben was taken aback for a few seconds. "That's a real sweet thing to say, Reece."

"You have that same quality. It's something you can kind of sense after being around you for a little while. I felt it when I met you on the stairs outside Roger's apartment. I know you were just doing your job, but you have this patience and kindness to you that makes me want to be near you."

"Well, like you said—I was just doing my job." Ben was a little too touched to articulate much else.

"No, you're a good guy. And I think you'll always have people in your life because of it." Reece smiled, then laughed quietly and rubbed the back of his neck. "But enough of the serious stuff. Let's watch Jimmy Stewart and Hitchcock at their best."

THEY'D gotten settled comfortably on the couch. Ben had held his arm open, and Reece had slotted himself against Ben's side. He could smell Ben, could feel the heat of him through his T-shirt. He'd commented that it had been a long time since he'd curled up to watch a movie with someone—that he'd always enjoyed that sort of closeness—and for some reason that seemed to please Ben, and he'd pulled Reece a little closer.

They'd actually made it through about fifteen minutes of the film, just enjoying it, chatting quietly. He was practically reclined alongside Ben, tucked up snugly against him with the man's arm around him. Ben's thumb had been softly rubbing back and forth over the same spot of his wrist, the soft touch lovely, but teasing.

Then he'd caught Ben's eye, and they'd reached for each other at the same time, their lips meeting with soft satisfied hums. Now he'd somehow been maneuvered to lie beneath Ben, the larger man careful not to let Reece carry his full weight—not that he couldn't take it, he was hardly a waif—but he appreciated Ben's consideration. And it had to be one of the most erotic things he'd ever seen, seeing Ben kneel up, their eye contact never breaking as he reached over his head and pulled his T-shirt off, tossing it on the floor.

"Christ, look at you."

Broad shoulders and thick biceps, strong flanks, a light dusting of dark hair, a flat, hard stomach and narrow hips. Absolutely gorgeous. His eyes were dilated and hungry, his lips swollen and moist. Reece sat up briefly, allowing his own shirt to be pulled over his head before being urged to lie back down with the press of Ben's chest against his.

"How do you make me want you so much?" Ben whispered into his ear, and Reece thought he might come right there.

Reece sighed Ben's name, arching his neck as Ben kissed a path toward his chest. He bit his lip—hard—when first one nipple, then the other was drawn into Ben's mouth to be sucked and bit teasingly. He hissed and pressed his head back onto the couch.

"Ben." His gasp had a hint of desperation to it, and he was distantly aware that his legs had drifted apart in welcome, his knees bending to accommodate Ben's hips. They ground together for a moment, the friction hot and good.

"Need more than this, Reece," Ben growled, "want to feel you moving beneath me, your legs wrapped around my waist. Want to hear you moan when I have you again and again…." He ground down hard with his words, pulling a ragged breath from Reece.

"Oh, fuck. Bed. Right fucking now, Ben. Bed!"

Ben pulled him upright, kissing him hard before quickly leading him to the stairs and up to the bedroom. As soon as they were near the bed, Ben urged him to lie down, and he pulled himself up toward the headboard as Ben followed him. Their kiss was hard and desperate, and Reece let out a little gasp as the button fly to his jeans was ripped open and his jeans and underwear were tugged down in a quick, hard tug. He bent his knees, and Ben pulled the jeans from his legs, tossing them aside before immediately diving back for another hungry kiss.

Reece groaned at the feel of Ben's still jeans-clad form against his naked skin. He broke the kiss and grabbed desperately for Ben's belt and fly. Ben leaned on both hands above him, watching as Reece tugged his jeans down enough to push his hand beneath his black briefs, sliding down past his cock to cup his balls. Ben hissed, his eyes closing.

Reece swallowed, leaning up on one hand so that he could brush his nose against Ben's and slowly kiss him while his hand started to jack him off.

"Ben?"

"Oh Christ." Ben opened his eyes and nearly groaned again. Reece looked so fucking hot, his lips moist, his dark eyes watching him as he stroked him off.

"Think you can get it up again if I take the edge off?"

"For you? *So* not a problem."

Reece grinned, bit his lip for a second, and then slowly pushed Ben to lie flat on the bed. He stretched out over him, kissing him leisurely. "Good." He pressed kisses along Ben's neck and said, "Wanna suck you."

"Fuck." Ben arched his neck, the words going straight to his groin. "God, do it. Suck me."

Reece pressed his lips against Ben's magnificent chest, nipping playfully at a nipple and grinning when Ben hissed. "Promise me you'll never wax." He ran his hands over the light dusting of hair. "I fucking love how masculine you are. Can be all sweet and shit, but fuck, you're all man. All fucking man."

Ben grinned, raising one arm to rest behind his head, his other hand touching Reece's cheek, his thumb rubbing over his bottom lip. "Anything you want."

Reece nipped at his thumb playfully. "Want you in my mouth, in *me*. Just need to know if I can suck you without a rubber, handsome. Don't mind using one, but I'd rather feel your skin on my tongue."

"It's been well over a year since my last partner, and I get tested every few months out of habit."

"Good. I'm moving 'you coming down my throat' into the safe category."

Ben groaned and pulled him down for a hard kiss. Reece grinned mischievously. "I'm good to go, too; won't fuck without a rubber, but otherwise your meat is mine."

Ben raised his knees as Reece slunk down to lie between them, his hips lifting a little at the first touch of Reece's hand. His eyes slid shut with a groan at the feel of Reece's mouth sucking on the head, taking in a little at a time until that dark head of hair began to bob and then went to town on him. "Oh shit, this might be short."

Ben leaned up on one elbow; he had to see this. His free hand wound its way into tousled brown hair, gripping slightly, guiding just a little as his hips began to meet every downward slide of that heavenly mouth.

Reece's arms hooked under his legs loosely and touched Ben's hips; he could tell the man was trying his best not to thrust too hard. He squeezed those hips, pulling them upwards, silently telling the man to enjoy it.

Ben groaned and suddenly lay back down, both of his hands wound tightly into Reece's hair as he guided his head down, his hips starting to pump up. He pressed his head back into the mattress as his balls began to draw up. He was not a small man, and he doubted anyone had ever been able to take care of his cock as well as Reece was now. "Fuck, soon."

Reece sucked harder, swirling his tongue and groaning when he could around the hard, hot dick in his mouth.

"Gonna come. Gonna come in that pretty mouth," Ben growled.

Christ, Reece was close himself, but he held off rubbing against the duvet. He wanted to save it for when Ben was ready to go again.

"Aw, fuck, Reece!"

The tight head in his mouth swelled and then pumped thick jets into his throat. Reece moaned around the mouthful, continuing to bob his head very slowly, swallowing it all and eventually allowing the large cock to slip from his lips. That had to be the best head he'd ever given: Ben looked stunned. His chest rose and fell rapidly and glistened with sweat, the light spread of dark hair slightly damp. His legs spread lazily and he was panting with one arm flung over his eyes.

Reece nuzzled against Ben's hip, pressing kisses along his stomach and over his heart until he came level with his face. With a kiss to Ben's cheek, he pulled his arm away and then kissed his mouth.

"I'll be doing that quite a bit in the future. Just so you know."

Ben gave a breathless little laugh that made Reece grin. "You have the most perfect mouth. Christ, no one's ever taken me in so deep before." His arm made its way around Reece, pulling him from above him down to his side.

"Their loss."

"C'mere." Ben's voice was husky, and his cock, which was still half hard, twitched against Reece's thigh as he rolled above him. "Sexy little shit," he said as he kissed along Reece's neck, making him sigh. "Making me come so hard my eyeballs nearly explode."

Reece snorted, raising one knee so he could stroke his calf along Ben's hip. "So, get your revenge."

"Intend to."

Ben began to slink down his body; Reece stopped him, pulled him back for a second. "Another time. I'm desperate here, Ben."

With a groan Ben took Reece's hand and wrapped it around his rapidly hardening cock, encouraging him to bring it fully back to life. He leaned over to the bedside drawer and yanked it open, rummaging for a second and then pulling out some lube and a foil wrapper.

He knelt back on his haunches and spread Reece's legs before yanking him closer by the backs of his knees. Reece gasped in surprise, then grinned sheepishly. Ben smirked—not unkindly—and set Reece's legs on either side of his thighs. "I'm going to make this so good for you."

"May have to take it a little easy at first, it's been a while."

"How long?" Ben uncapped the lube and spread a line along Reece's thigh. He coated his first two fingers, then, leaning forward on one hand, he gently began to massage the puckered entrance, drawing a shaky breath from his partner.

"About seven months, just give me a minute when you get going, that's all. Not going to hold you back—don't want you to."

Witness

Ben leaned forward, watching Reece's eyes close as he slid his first digit in slowly. He kissed him deeply as he began to pump that finger, and then he gradually added another, scissoring them.

Reece whimpered into the kiss, raising his hips and gripping Ben's arm. "More."

Soon Ben was watching three fingers slowly move in and out of that tight hole. "Can't wait to be inside you."

"I'm too fucking close, *shit!*" Reece raised his hips in a rolling rhythm, pushing himself down on Ben's hand. "Fuck, now, Ben, please."

Ben tore open the foil with his teeth, then gently pulled his fingers free and rolled on the condom. He lifted up Reece's legs to rest over his hips and let the head of his hard dick rub teasingly over that tight entrance for a second before pushing through. He went slowly, groaning when he felt Reece's ankles lock at the small of his back, pulling him all the way in.

"Fuck, that's a tight fit."

Reece was panting. "What I said about taking it easy? Forget it." He squeezed, pulling a growl from Ben. "Fuck me."

"I will, just give yourself a second."

Ben held himself up on his hands, leaning down for a slow kiss as his hips began to roll. His movements, graceful at first, became a little rougher, deeper, until eventually he was holding himself up with one arm while lifting Reece's hip to meet his every thrust with the other.

"Fuck, oh fucking Christ, yes. There! Right... *there!*"

Reece started to lose it. He dragged Ben down to him, clamping his legs tightly around his waist and gripping the man's back desperately as Ben began to pound into him, to ride him in earnest.

Every thrust became fantastically jarring, Reece's steady litany of curses tapering off into grunts and moans of pleasure. He pushed his head back into the mattress and his hands up against Ben's chest. Ben allowed Reece to push him away and leaned up, grinning as Reece ran his hands over his chest—he seemed to have a thing for it—then let them rest at Ben's hips.

"So good, oh shit, gonna shoot… Ben!"

That tight heat around him became vice-like, and then Reece was coming, spraying between them, arching his back beautifully.

Ben stilled his movements and ran a hand over the panting man's slick belly, up his chest, and then cupped the side of his face, letting his thumb push its way gently between his lips for Reece to suck clean. "So not done yet." He pulled out gently, then rolled Reece onto his stomach. "And neither are you," he growled into his ear, not pulling Reece to his knees but instead spreading his thighs and cheeks apart, and pushing back in. He stretched over Reece and pushed his upper body up with his hands resting on either side of Reece's shoulders.

"Fuck." Reece could only gasp as Ben steadily began to fuck him again, grinding into him. He thought distantly that no one got this lucky. That this sweet, smart, fucking gorgeous guy was also a dream in the bedroom? Just too good to be true.

"Christ, Ben… you're just… fucking *owning* me." Reece could suddenly feel Ben's breath by his ear.

"Making you mine."

Reece called out when that first hard, jarring thrust slid across his gland, waking his cock right the fuck back up. He spread his legs as far as he could and raised his hips up off the bed, offering himself wide open. "Fuck, oh shit, oh fuck." He could hear Ben's breathless laugh behind him but so did not give a shit at that point.

"Don't stop, please, God…."

With a strength that was arousing as fuck, Ben pulled him onto his knees, and he scrambled to catch himself with his hands. A hand locked on his shoulder and hip, and Ben went to town on his ass. When that hand slid from his hip around to his dick, he was a goner. He yelled Ben's name, jerking into his hand, and was left shaking completely apart. He felt Ben's rhythm stutter, and after a few more rough thrusts, he heard Ben yell for him, and then a pulsing warmth in his ass. Ben collapsed on his shoulder, out of breath and heavy as fuck. After a few moments, however, Ben seemed to remember himself and slowly lifted onto his hands. Holding the sides of the condom, he pulled out carefully.

"Ah shit."

"What's wrong?" Reece murmured. He felt kind of sleepy and his voice sounded a little hoarse.

"The condom split."

Reece looked over his shoulder, then rolled slowly over onto his back. He didn't know how he felt about that. He'd never let someone come in his ass before, accidentally or no. He held his breath so as to not gasp when he felt a slight stickiness between his thighs.

Ben got up to get rid of the condom, and when he came back he sat besides Reece, resting his arm over his head, and touched his cheek gently. "Hey, you okay?"

"Yeah, that's just never happened before. It's alright though. You tell me you're clean, I trust you."

"You shouldn't have to, but I promise you, you have nothing to worry about."

Reece felt suddenly a little shy of the man, which was fucking ridiculous considering five minutes ago....

"Hey, I'm sorry; I shouldn't have been so rough."

Reece laughed, "Don't apologize, that was by the far the single most intense fuck I have ever had." And didn't *that* just leave him all exposed and shit.

Ben smiled, then leaned down and kissed him slowly. "Wait here." He went to the bathroom, and Reece heard the water running. Ben came back with a damp cloth and wiped Reece clean. His touch was tender and very much appreciated; Reece couldn't help but flush a little when Ben wiped the cloth quickly between his thighs. But if Ben wasn't embarrassed, then why should he be? This kind of tenderness? It'd never been there for him before—afterward. Not with anyone he'd been with.

"How about a little dessert?" Ben asked.

Reece raised an eyebrow. "You got some stamina, cowboy; I'm down for the count tonight."

Ben grinned and swatted at his leg. "Fine, you don't want any of my blueberry pie, more for me." He began to climb off the bed and laughed when Reece lunged for his wrist.

"No, no, no. Wait," Reece laughed. "There's always room for pie." He began to follow, but Ben shook his head.

"Get comfy. It's late—screw the crumbs, we'll eat in bed."

"Alright." Reece grinned almost impishly as he pushed the quilt down with his feet and climbed in, snuggling down and resting his hands behind his head. He watched Ben leave the room and relaxed against the pillows. Wow. That's all there was to say, really. That had been a lay for the books. Though it didn't feel like just a fuck. Usually right about now he'd be either reading too much into it, or wanting to make his exit, but he didn't want to get away from Ben. More importantly, Ben didn't seem to want to get away from him, despite the condom thing, which had weirded him out a lot less than he ever thought it might. He ran his hands over his face tiredly and smiled to himself. This guy was a keeper; he'd have to do his best not to fuck it up.

Ben ambled downstairs, naked as the day he was born. He cut two slices of pie and set them in bowls with forks. He'd been worried for a second, there. He'd never had a condom rip on him before; Reece had looked a little surprised but seemed okay about it. Perhaps he'd go for a different brand next time.

He caught his reflection in the kitchen window and grinned suddenly, licking berry juice from his thumb. He had no idea where

Witness

that had suddenly come from—flipping Reece over and making him come again. The guy had been just so sexy, so much fun, so open and generous with that mouth of his. He didn't know where this thing with Reece was going, but he hoped it'd lead to more than mind-blowing sex. He liked the guy—had fun with him.

Walking back into the bedroom, he paused and then smiled. He set the bowls down on the nightstand quietly, pulled back the sheets, and slid carefully into bed, mindful not to wake Reece up. He got comfortable, reached to turn off the lamp, and curled himself around his sleeping partner.

Reece hummed in his sleep, and Ben smiled tenderly as the man snuggled close to him, burrowing right up into his arms, his head on Ben's shoulder, tucked under his chin, as if it were the most comfortable place in the world. Ben fell asleep just like that, holding him close.

CHAPTER 6

MAN, was he going to spoil his cop tonight. Reece pulled on his brakes and then tucked his bike under the porch of Ben's house. He was supposed to be seeing him later that night, but Darren had told him to go celebrate his sale with Ben, so he thought he'd surprise him.

He'd sold a photo. It was nothing overly artistic or too amazing, just an old man sitting on a bench feeding some ducks. The photo wasn't new, either; he'd taken it a couple of years ago when wandering through a park with his camera and had gotten lucky. The lighting, shadow, even the fucking ducks were perfect. He'd always kind of liked it; there was something peaceful about it. Now it would be used for a life insurance leaflet. And he felt pretty goddamn good about that. It turned out that pimping his portfolio out to magazines and design companies did occasionally pay off.

He'd thought that perhaps he'd have to sit and wait on the porch for Ben to finish his shift, but apparently he was already home, if the truck in the drive was anything to go by. He knocked on the door and waited. After a little while, with no answer, he looked at the truck in the drive and knocked again. Could he let himself in? They'd been seeing each other for a couple of weeks now, but were they at that place yet? Would it seem presumptuous?

He opened the door and poked his head in, calling for Ben. When he still got no answer, he let himself in and closed the door behind him. That was weird, usually Ben answered right away. He'd certainly never leave the door unlocked if he was out.

Witness

"Ben?"

He walked through the living room and kitchen, dumping his backpack with a change of clothes inside on the counter. He'd need to hang that stuff up if he wanted to wear it out tonight. He realized that he could have just called Ben and asked him to pick him up later, but he'd been so delighted with the news that the first thing he'd wanted to do was tell Ben, so he'd gone home to collect a few thing for the night and headed straight over to his house.

A clinking noise drew his attention through the kitchen to the garage. He knocked on the door and opened it slowly, putting his head through first.

"Ben? Ben, are you in he—"

He stopped short. No wonder Ben hadn't heard him. He appeared to be deep in concentration as he lay back on his weight bench, lifting a bar that looked like it weighed more than a small pony. Good God, the man was beautiful. The corded muscles in his forearms strained as he pushed the bar up, where he then let out a breath, and lowered the bar again. Sweat glistened on his bare chest, over his brow and forearms, and Reece was distantly aware that he should probably let Ben know he was there, rather than just watching him like some pervert. But he wasn't sure how to interrupt him without surprising the man while he was obviously concentrating. Not to mention that Reece was pretty sure he'd forgotten how to speak.

The problem solved itself when after a few more lifts, Ben rested the bar, and sat up. He spotted Reece and a delighted smile spread across his lips.

"Hey, what are you doing here?"

Reece watched as Ben snagged a towel from the floor, stood, and swiped it over the back of his neck and chest. It took Reece a few seconds to realize it was his turn to talk.

"Uh, I had some good news today and wanted to come straight over to surprise you when you got in and"—he paused to swallow as he watched a bead of sweat disappear into the fabric of Ben's low riding shorts, "I hope you don't mind," he said, throwing his thumb over his shoulder. "I knocked but you didn't answer, and I saw your truck so...."

Ben pulled him closer to kiss him, but kept a small distance between their bodies. "'Course I don't mind. Feel free to do that anytime." He was still a little out of breath.

Reece managed to nod. "Ben. Christ, look at you."

Ben blinked in surprise, then gave a small self-conscious laugh and shrugged. "You caught me unawares."

"I can see that."

Reece reached for another kiss, wrapping his hands around those hard biceps to pull Ben close. "C'mere."

"Oh, hey...." Ben shied away. "I'm all sweaty."

"Yeah, and it's fucking hot."

Reece pulled him back down for a deep kiss, and hummed happily as those strong arms held him close. "Don't know if you noticed," Reece said between kisses, "but I may have a thing for these muscles."

"You don't say."

"Never did before, you know. You've turned me into some shallow twink."

Ben smiled and pulled away from the kiss. He cupped the slightly shorter man's face, letting his thumbs run over his cheeks. "You're not shallow. And you're definitely not some twink."

Reece ran his hands over Ben's firm chest; he could feel himself beginning to harden. He tilted his head up for another kiss. "What are you doing back early anyhow?"

"A work thing." Ben wrapped one arm around Reece's neck, angling down for another kiss. "We had a jumper today, had to pull him back."

Witness

Reece pulled back immediately, his erection sputtering to an abrupt halt. "What? Are you okay?"

Ben sighed, "Yeah, I'm fine, but they sent me home early anyway. It's no big deal."

Reece stepped back a little. "No big deal?"

"The guy's fine, I'm fine—"

"Tell me what happened."

Ben raised a brow at the demand, not sure if he found it annoying or endearing. "There was a jumper, top floor of an apartment building. I was one of the first to the scene; the guy was having some sort of nervous breakdown. I managed to cajole him away from the ledge, but he lost his footing and I had to grab him. I caught him, and one of the other officers managed to grab me before I fell too. I'm okay."

"That's... I—"

"Look," Ben said, pulling back, "it's my job, Reece, this stuff happens."

Reece frowned. "I know that."

"Do you? I don't just answer calls to lonely old people, you know—changing light bulbs and fishing electric toothbrushes out of toilets."

Reece stared. "You've lost me."

Ben sighed again. It always got in the way eventually. "My job gets a little dangerous sometimes." He tried to pass his voice off as casual. "Can you tell me if it's going to be a problem?"

Now Reece was even more confused. "What do you mean a prob—oh." Understanding dawned on him. "Oh, no, I wasn't getting angry or anything."

"Then what were you going to say?"

Reece shrugged, suddenly feeling rather small. "Just... that that's pretty amazing. You saving someone's life and all." He frowned. "You're job's affected relationships for you before, I'm gathering."

Ben shrugged. "More like it's stopped things from developing into anything permanent."

"I see. Well"—he touched his hands to Ben's hips, moving close—"their loss is my gain."

"You say that now."

"Hey." He gave Ben a little shake, making the man meet his eyes. "I get that being a cop is part of who you are, that it's in your blood practically. I couldn't get angry at you for something I respect you for. Can't promise I won't worry, but I wouldn't want to change you."

When Ben didn't answer he continued quietly. "Ben, I'll take you any way I can get you. I'm not going to suddenly decide I can't hack it. I want to be with you." He gave a small, crooked smile and said, "I'm kind of crazy about you."

Ben smiled hesitantly, his voice soft. "Yeah?"

Reece nodded and pulled the larger man into a hug, then leaned back to look him in the eye. "Yes. Now can I suggest we fuck or something before we both turn into women?"

Ben laughed, seeming more like himself. "Sounds good to me. Oh, hey—what was the good news?"

"Hmm?" Reece had gotten sidetracked again by the pretty skin.

Ben grinned, apparently aware of the effect he was having on him. "Your good news, why you came here?"

"Oh, that. Seems kind of dumb now."

Ben gave him a quick squeeze. "Don't be stupid, tell me."

"Um, well I sold a picture."

"Yeah?" Ben smiled brightly. He seemed delighted for him, and Reece felt some of the proud glow from before worm its way back.

"Yeah, it's for this brochure thing for life insurance," he said, shrugging.

"That's great!"

Reece grinned and ran the back of his fingers over Ben's stomach. "Thanks, doesn't mean I'm rich or anything, just means I have a little more cash this month than usual. I know you were coming over later, but I thought perhaps I could take my guy out for a meal, my treat."

Ben smirked. "Your guy, huh?"

Reece fought the flush he felt rising and yanked playfully at Ben's waist. "Yeah, my guy. And we definitely have to go out now." He touched Ben's chest softly. "I have to celebrate my boyfriend being a hero, now don't I?"

Ben looked at him for a moment and then leaned that short distance down to kiss him hard. "We're celebrating for you too." He gave Reece a quick squeeze and pulled away. He walked backward to the garage door, a grin playing on his lips. "I need a shower, especially if we're going out."

Reece sighed; he'd wanted to fool around a little. "Okay."

Ben got to the door and then looked at him expectantly. "Well, you gonna come scrub my back or what?"

"Okay!"

Ben snorted as he was rushed out of the garage and up the stairs.

"I SAID I'd buy you a new shower curtain."

Ben couldn't help but chuckle. He sat back when the waiter appeared with their food. Up until then they'd both taken turns paying when going out, but always at reasonably priced restaurants. Reece had picked a real swanky restaurant—it certainly wasn't cheap—and he'd only been there once before himself. He knew this was Reece's treat, but he also knew that he wasn't the richest man on the planet. It didn't make him think any less of Reece for it; it just made him aware to be sensitive to the fact that being able to treat him in a place like this meant something to Reece. All the same, he'd picked one of the middle-priced dishes, and smiled when Reece had spoken over him and ordered two of the fattest steaks the restaurant had, along with the house wine.

"I know what you're doing and I think you're a sweetheart for it, but it's my treat, remember?" Reece had said.

Ben waited for the waiter to leave and picked up the conversation where they'd left it as he shook out his napkin and laid it over his lap.

"I'm not saying it wasn't worth it."

They'd gotten a little energetic earlier on in the shower. It hadn't ended exactly how he'd planned but it had certainly been funny as hell. There'd been a flailing of limbs grabbing for purchase and the ripping of the shower curtain on hooks. They'd ended up on the bathroom floor—which had nearly flooded—soaked and sudsy as hell, laughing like a pair of lunatics.

"We'll take a bath next time." Reece cut into his steak and winked.

"Perhaps we should avoid the bathroom altogether?"

"No way, I love how you look all soapy."

Ben shook his head and dug in. "This is good."

"Mm, we'll have to come here on special occasions or something."

"Like what?" Ben smiled; he was interested to know what special occasions they'd be spending together. Reece seemed to realize his faux pas and swallowed his food as a slight blush crept up his neck.

"Well, uh, when I sell a picture. Or whenever you go all 'Officer Ben to the rescue'."

"Uh huh." He wasn't letting Reece off that lightly.

Witness

"Easter?" Reece offered.

Ben chuckled.

"Public holidays?"

Ben was laughing quietly now, and Reece seemed to relax a little. His voice was a little tentative when he next spoke. "Maybe… Christmas or New Year's?"

Ben put down his fork and reached across the table to stroke the back of Reece's hand. "We can do that."

Reece's smile upped its wattage. "Good."

"Ben?"

They both looked up at the man now standing beside their table. He was tall, as tall as Ben. He had short blond hair, wide shoulders, and was wearing a suit that probably cost more than Reece made in a mo— hang on one fucking minute.

Reece shifted uncomfortably in his seat as Ben stood up rather awkwardly when the guy insisted on giving him a hug. This was the asshole who had yelled at him in the foyer of that office building around a month ago. God, had he laid into him, and in front of an audience too. How the fuck did he know Ben?

"Ah, Reece, this is Jason. An old friend."

Uh huh. Code for ex-boyfriend. Shit.

"Jason, Reece."

The asshole held his hand out for Reece to shake, and Reece took it. He felt his stomach turn a little when the grip on his hand tightened a fraction, and the guy tilted his head and squinted at him in recognition.

"Have we met?"

"Nope. Don't think so."

A slow smile slid across the guy's handsome face. "Yeah, sure we have, you're one of those guys who delivers stuff on a bike, right?"

"A bike messenger," Reece said quietly.

"Right. Well, small world."

"You two know each other?" Ben seemed to become more uncomfortable by the second as he sat back down.

"We might have had a tiny bit of an altercation a while back," Jason said.

Reece sputtered. "Altercation? You fucking howled at me in front of a room full of people."

Jason held his hands up in an innocent gesture "Whoa there, I'm sorry, I didn't mean to upset you." He put his hands back in his pockets and gave Ben a crooked smile, as if sharing a joke with him at the expense of the highly strung guy who delivered stuff on a bike.

Great. Now I look like an asshole.

"I apologize for my poor manners. I'm a partner in that firm, you see and, well, those papers you 'misplaced' were very important, Ryan."

"It's Reece," Reece spat back, looking to Ben for support and getting more pissed off by the second when it didn't seem to be coming.

"I'm sorry. *Reece.*"

"Jason, Reece and I are here *together*," Ben said. "Could you please mind the way you speak to him?"

About fucking time. Take that, you corporate prick.

"Oh, hey, looks like I've made a bad impression. Ben," he said, turning to look at Ben with a smarmy come-hither smile dripping from his lips, "I just wanted to say that you were pretty incredible today. I saw you on the news."

"The news?" That made Reece blink. "I didn't know you were on the news."

Witness

Ben shrugged uncomfortably. "It's not like the cameras were on me, they were on the guy I was trying to drag back inside the building."

"Still as strong as I remember." Jason nudged Ben's shoulder playfully.

Reece frowned. *Did that asshole just wink at my boyfriend?*

"Look, uh, it was just lovely meeting you, but we were having a private—"

Up went those fucking hands again. "Oh, I'm sorry, say no more. I'm actually here with a client myself and couldn't believe my luck seeing Ben again. Say, you remember when we came here a while back? I thought you didn't like this place too much?"

And there it went: all the wind left Reece's sails. He officially felt two inches tall.

Ben shot an apologetic glance at Reece before turning back to Jason. "You remember wrong."

"Well, it was a while ago. Anyway, I'll let you two get back to your food. Here..."

He reached into his suit pocket and pulled out one of those sterling silver cases used to hold business cards. Reece had wanted one of those for his Reece's Family Portraits cards but had thought it a frivolous use of his limited funds.

"Here's my card, we should get together sometime. You have a birthday coming up soon, don't you? Let's go for drinks."

Reece couldn't think of a thing to say. It was beyond uncomfortable. Ben took the card but placed it on the table. "That's a nice idea, but I have plans."

"Another time, then."

Ben gave Jason a strained smile but otherwise said nothing. Jason turned to Reece and nodded, then left for his own table. The silence between them was tense for a few seconds before Ben attempted to lighten the mood. "Well, this is a little awkward." *And just a couple of minutes ago...*

"Your ex-boyfriend is an asshole."

"Yep, couldn't agree more."

At least that was something. Reece shifted in his seat and picked up his knife and fork, though he found that his appetite had disappeared. He just wanted to go home. Alone. He felt fucking pathetic.

"I wouldn't have minded," he said softly, trying to hide how crushed he actually felt. He'd loved the idea of bringing Ben to this place, ordering a big bottle of wine and the most expensive meal on the menu for him. "We could have gone somewhere else."

Ben's hand reached across the table and lay across his own. "I do like this place. I liked it before. It was the company I didn't care for."

Reece gave a small smile. Internally his mind was racing for something to say to get the night back on track. Ben interrupted his thoughts.

"You're not hungry anymore?" He seemed a little sad.

"Um, no, I don't think so. But you go on ahead and finish."

"Why don't we get out of here?"

Reece put down his cutlery and laid his napkin across the plate. He signaled to a waiter and asked for the bill. When they were alone again, waiting for the bill, he sighed, looking apologetically at the man opposite him.

"I got an advance payment on the photo I sold today, and the first thing I wanted to do was find you and spoil you. Make you feel as special as you make me feel."

Ben was more than a little touched; he squeezed Reece's hand. "You do."

Reece paid the bill, and they left. The car journey was a little more quiet than usual.

"It's really beginning to pour." Reece remarked.

"Yeah, I'm pretty sure I heard a few rumbles of thunder too."

It was quiet again for a few moments before Reece finally blurted out what he wanted to ask. "You have a birthday coming up, then? I don't even know how old you are."

"I'll be thirty-five in a few weeks. How about you, when's yours?"

"End of July. It'll be the big three-O for me."

"Hey, a milestone."

"Yeah. So...." Reece rubbed his hands over his thighs. "You have plans? Going away for your birthday?" He spoke evenly enough, but the unsure note as to whether he'd be welcome was painfully apparent.

Ben reached over and squeezed his knee. "You tell me, handsome, what do you want to do?"

"Oh, you were... oh, okay." Reece actually smiled at that, not caring how simple it may have made him look. He suddenly felt foolish for thinking that Ben would have made plans without him. "Well, you'll be the birthday boy, you should choose."

Ben thought for a moment, leaning forward and looking up when a streak of lightning lit the sky. "Actually, you know what I'd like?"

"What?"

"I'd like a quiet night in with you, and my closest friends. Just you and me, a bottle of wine, good food and good company. And you can meet Ted and Sharon; they're like family to me."

"That sounds nice." Reece smiled. *Meeting his family.*

"Yeah? Not... boring or anything?" The recent run-in with Jason had apparently unearthed a few insecurities of his own.

Reece frowned. "No, not at all. I kind of like it when we stay in and do simple stuff like that." He smiled crookedly. "I'm not really into the going out—the bar and club scene—anymore. I like when we go to the movies or stay in. I like watching you cook, then helping you with the dishes. If that makes you boring, then I guess I am too."

Ben was pretty sure right then that he was in love with Reece. But saying it right after running into Jason didn't feel quite right, as if he were trying to compensate for how the asshole had made Reece feel.

"And I'd be very happy to meet your family, Ben."

There was sincerity in his voice that struck a chord with Ben; he squeezed Reece's knee again before putting both hands back onto the steering wheel and decided at the last moment to take a left as opposed to the right as he usually would. He grinned.

"Hey, are we going a different way home—to your house, I mean?"

Ben grinned. He'd heard the slip-up. "Nope, we're going somewhere else instead."

"Ben, it's torrential outside, where could you possibly want to go?"

Ben wouldn't explain until they had parked. They were on a side road somewhere, surrounded by trees. Ahead, Reece could see a small clearing with a stream. Ben grinned and leaned his arm on the back of Reece's headrest.

"Where are we?" Reece asked.

"Well, now it's just a forgotten side road not used by anyone. Around twenty years ago, it was the most popular make-out spot any teenager could wish for."

Reece blinked. "You brought me here to make out?" The idea tickled him, and he burst into laughter. Ben smiled; that'd been the desired reaction.

"When I was fifteen I came here once, on a double date with my buddy Tom. He sat in the front making out with his girlfriend, and I sat in the back with her friend, making awkward conversation and trying to think of a good excuse not to kiss her without hurting her feelings."

Witness

Reece snorted, "Let me guess... Tom?"

"Had no idea how much I wished it was me up there in front with him."

Reece looked at him for a second, just smiling, then he unbuckled his seatbelt, and in a rather graceful move managed to turn and straddle Ben's lap. The fit was a little tight in the front seat, but with his head bent, he had just enough room. He touched both hands to Ben's face, gently cupping it as he kissed him slowly.

"I'll be Tom for you." He brushed his nose alongside Ben's in a tender gesture.

"I'd rather you be Reece."

Reece kissed him deeply before pulling away and grinning impishly. "Let's get in the back seat. More room."

Then he was scrambling off Ben's lap, and out of the door. Ben laughed and unbuckled, following him. Lightning flashed overhead as they dived for the backseat. In the few seconds they'd been outside, they got damn near drenched. Both laughed in plain old carefree amusement, and immediately began to pull at each other's clothes.

"Ever had sex in the back of a car?"

"What kind of slut do you take me for, Ben Jenkins?"

Ben nuzzled into his neck as he pulled at Reece's pants. "The kind who's about to ride my cock in a thunderstorm."

Reece shuddered. "Oh, hell yes. Lie on your back, I'm leading."

Ben laughed and lay down on his back, shimmying his jeans down to his knees with Reece's help. Reece straddled him naked, lying flat against Ben to kiss him hard.

"Long shot, but... any lube in here?"

"Um, don't laugh, but I have some hand cream somewhere in the front."

Reece raised an eyebrow.

"Shut up!" Ben laughed, "My hands get a little dry in the winter when I'm driving."

"Man, you are so gay."

"Says the man about to impale himself on my dick."

Reece laughed. "Touché."

He leaned over the front seat, searching for the hand cream. He dug his wallet out of his discarded pants and pulled out a condom. Thunder rolled outside and lightning momentarily lit up the trees outside the car as Reece rolled the condom on Ben's cock.

"Are you sure this isn't breaking some law, Officer?"

"I don't intend on arresting either of us so don't worry yourself and get lubed up. I'm as hard as nails for you here, Reece."

Ben's breath came a little quicker and his cock throbbed in Reece's hand. Reece closed his eyes, leaned forward, and reached around to prepare himself.

"Shit," Ben whispered, "I bet you don't have the first clue how irresistible you are, do you?"

Reece panted a little, scissoring his fingers the best he could inside of himself as Ben's hands stroked his thighs.

"As long as you're interested, that's all that matters."

"I'm interested. I'm fucking obsessed."

Reece moaned and pulled his fingers free. "That'll have to do. Want you *now*."

The only sounds to be heard were of the wind howling outside, the rain hammering down on the windshield, and harsh breathing as Reece lowered himself—with help—onto Ben's dick. Lightning flashed, and Ben's breath caught at the concentration on Reece's features, the complete rapture and single focus.

They both groaned when Reece's behind met the bristles of Ben's pubic hair. He rested his hands flat on Ben's chest, trusting that he wouldn't hurt the man if he needed to support himself, and closed his eyes as he concentrated on starting the familiar rhythm.

Ben bent his knees and wrapped his hands around Reece's hips, helping him with the upward lift and downward slide. Reece's head hung forward so as not to hit the roof of the car, his eyes focused on Ben's lust-filled gaze as he picked up the pace, beginning to bounce, squeezing his muscles and fucking himself on Ben's cock.

"That's it, baby," Ben whispered. "You fuck yourself on me. Feel me all the way inside."

"Oh, God," Reece gasped.

"You've no idea," Ben growled, "no idea what it does to me; how fucking possessive it makes me feel to see you bouncing on my cock."

He began to move his hips up in sharp, erratic moves, ringing choked-off cries of surprised, helpless pleasure from the slighter man. The truck was rocking, he could feel it. Reece's actions were getting more exaggerated.

"Oh God. Oh fuck, oh god, Ben. You're so fucking hard inside me, so fucking hard."

"Christ," Ben panted, "God, I gotta come...."

"Oh fuck, Ben... *Ben!*" Reece rolled his hips frantically, slamming himself down onto Ben, then squeezing as he pulled up. Ben's hands tightened on his hips, guiding him frantically up and down. Thunder roared outside, just overhead. Lightning flashed again, and Reece threw his head back, yelling Ben's name as he came over his stomach and chest.

Ben held his breath when the truck was filled with light from the storm at the same time Reece yelled in absolute fucking ecstasy and came in thick spurts. He pushed up into Reece's quivering passage and shuddered as he filled the condom, his cry nearly drowned out by the crash and bang of thunder.

Reece collapsed forward, Ben's arms wound possessively around him, and they lay gasping for breath, clutching each other close. The storm moved on after a little while, rumbling in the distance, and the only noise to be heard was once again the whistle and rustle of the wind through the trees, the heavy pattering of the rain and their labored breathing. Ben ran his hands along Reece's sides and back, keeping him there.

"Changed my mind." Reece murmured eventually, sounding sleepy despite the awkward position.

"About what?"

"This is what we should do on special occasions."

CHAPTER 7

"THESE are amazing, Reece."

Ben lay reclined against Reece's headboard, naked except for the sheets bunched around his waist and the portfolio in his lap.

"You just want to get laid again," Reece called from his bathroom.

Ben grinned but shook his head as he turned another page of one of the massive portfolios Reece had brought to show him. They were beautiful, intriguing, some of them sad, but all amazing. At least to him. He couldn't imagine why anyone wouldn't want to buy Reece's photos; he would. But then, he was biased.

"I'm pretty sure I don't have to flatter you to get a repeat performance."

It had been a long time since he'd let another guy top him. But when they'd been kissing in his bed, slowly undressing, he'd felt Reece's hands stray downward to caress his behind, a question rather than a grope. He'd raised a brow, and Reece had asked the question.

"Let me?" His voice husky and his eyes most definitely smoldering.

And Ben had found that rather than just letting Reece take control, he'd actually wanted him to. And goddamn but it had felt right. It'd never been his favorite thing, but he'd never been head over heels for any of the guys he'd slept with. He felt that perhaps he was a top by nature, but sharing himself with his lover like that was something he would never deny Reece, or himself, in the future.

"Hmm."

Ben looked up to see Reece standing in the bathroom doorway, naked, rubbing a towel over his damp hair and looking at him.

"I like it when you're naked. You should stay like that. Naked. And in my bed."

Ben grinned. "I'd have to leave at some point."

"No. I wouldn't let you."

Ben raised an eyebrow. "And how would you manage that, Tiny?"

Reece sputtered in indignation, throwing the towel at him. "Hey, I'm average height and size, you're just freakin' huge." He crossed his arms and leaned against the door frame with a pout. "And as for calling a guy Tiny when he's standing in front of you naked—that's just cruel."

Ben snorted and moved the portfolio to the side, holding his arm out and gesturing for Reece to come forward. "Come here."

Reece stayed put and turned his head petulantly to one side.

"Come here, you huge fucking stud."

Reece grinned and climbed onto the bed. "That's better." He pulled the sheets back and climbed in next to Ben. "And in answer to your question, I'd keep you here by tying you to my bed. Or cuffing you. I know where to get my hands on a pair, so be careful."

Ben laughed and pulled him close. They dropped down against the pillows and cuddled up close. Ben snorted as he curled himself around Reece, pulling the man's back against his chest.

"I feel like I'm playing hooky," Ben said.

"You are, kind of." Reece chuckled.

"My shift would have ended round about now anyway, and I really did have a personal emergency."

"Personal emergency? Bunking off early to screw your brains out with your boyfriend counts as an emergency?"

"Yes. Though if work asks, the neighbors called to tell me they could smell gas, or Muddles needed to go to the vet, or something."

"I think I'm a bad influence on you." Reece turned and burrowed his way into Ben's arms.

"I think you've had a pretty good effect on me, actually," Ben murmured, kissing the top of his head. "Though lying naked in bed at six in the evening seems a bit indulgent."

"That's what I'm here for, to bring indulgence, fun, and cycling shorts into your life."

Ben chuckled. "I love being here," he said quietly, and then suddenly he felt a little vulnerable at having said so.

Reece smiled softly and then scooted a fraction closer, so their heads were on the same pillow, and gave him a brief kiss. "Love having you here." His hand found Ben's, and entwined their fingers. "Have to say, though; I was a little hesitant to have you over."

"Why?"

Reece shrugged. "Not the way to go if I want to impress a guy—showing him the hole I live in." He laughed a little but there wasn't much humor in it.

Ben frowned. "This place isn't a hole. It's a home."

"No, your place is a home."

"No, my place is a house."

Reece frowned but Ben simply shook his head and continued. "There's nothing wrong with your apartment."

"It's not so bad, I guess. I've been living here since I moved here when I was nineteen. Ten years. I guess…." He took a deep breath and let it out in a sigh. "I guess I just expected to be somewhere else by now."

"You mean living somewhere else?" Ben asked softly.

"Just, somewhere else in general." Reece shook his head and laughed at himself. "Ignore me, I can be an ungrateful shit sometimes."

He looked at Ben for a second, then, pulling him by the back of the neck, he kissed him firmly. After, he leaned his brow against Ben's and closed his eyes. "I'm glad you're here," he said in an almost whisper. He seemed to be debating something before he looked Ben in the eye with what seemed uncertainty. "Maybe you'd like a key? You wouldn't have to buzz in like everyone else."

A slow smile began to spread over Ben's lips, and he was about to whole-heartedly accept when said buzzer interrupted him. They both jumped slightly, then laughed.

"Hold that thought, I'll just go answer that."

Ben watched as Reece slipped into his boxers, and, with a mischievous grin, looked back at Ben before picking up his discarded uniform shirt and slipping it on. Ben winked at him, letting him know he liked it, and then rolled onto his back when Reece left and rubbed his hands over his face as he grinned widely. *Man, you got it bad.*

He was startled as Reece rushed back a few moments later, pulling back the sheets and picking Ben's underwear and trousers up off the floor and thrusting them at him.

"Up, up!" he urged.

"What the hell?"

"Oh crap, my place is a mess."

"Reece, what's going on?"

He was pulling on his pants as he watched Reece pulling clothes out of a drawer, searching for something to wear himself. Reece's back straightened when there was a knock at the door, and he turned to Ben with an almost hysterical laugh.

"Um. I wanted to ask you something else. I wasn't planning on laying it all on you tonight, after the key thing... don't want you getting scared off or anything...."

"*Reece*, what's going on?" Ben asked and gestured for the shirt Reece was wearing.

Reece looked down at himself and slipped the shirt off, handing it to Ben. The guy looked like a nervous wreck.

Reece seemed to hold his breath before blurting it out. "You wanna meet my parents?"

Ben paused, and a silly smile threatened to spread across his lips. "You want to introduce me to your parents?"

Reece winced when there was a second knock at the door. "Well, I've never actually brought anyone home before, you know? And, ah, well I think we've got something really special here and...." He pulled up his pants, looking panicked before seeming to give up and shrug, smiling at Ben. "Yeah, I'd like you to meet them." He snorted in amusement. "Please don't think I'm a freak."

Ben smiled and began to step forward to hug him. "Why would I think that, I'd love to—"

"Because that's them at the door."

Ben stopped dead, Reece's behavior suddenly making sense. Ben looked down at himself and began to quickly search for his socks with a curse while Reece laughed.

"I know, I swear I didn't know they were coming. They thought they'd *surprise* me because I hadn't made it home the other weekend. That, and they haven't been to visit me in so long...."

There was another knock at the door, this one sounding impatient. "I'd better let them in before my dad takes the hinges off the door." Reece began to leave and then stopped, his hand resting on the doorjamb. "He makes furniture by the way. His name's Allan and my mother's name is Marie." He left and went to answer the door, hoping his apartment didn't smell like sex.

Ben tucked his shirt in hastily, suddenly wishing he had something to wear other than his uniform. What if they thought he and Reece had some weird dress-up thing going on? He heard Reece open the door.

He listened to them greet each other first, waiting for when it seemed appropriate to leave the bedroom—the fucking *bedroom*.

"Mom, Dad, hi. Come on in." Reece gave them both a brief hug and led them into his tiny living room. "The place is a bit of a mess at the minute, I had no idea...."

"Well, we haven't been to see you in so long, we thought we'd come to you for a change," Reece's mother said.

"How's the work going?" his dad asked.

Reece was about to answer when a small thump and a muffled curse came from the bedroom. His father looked into the direction of his bedroom and then raised an eyebrow in question. Reece could swear the man was trying not to grin.

"Oh I'm sorry, sweetheart, you have—you have company?" his mother asked with a little more excitement in her voice than he cared for.

"Well, actually, I was planning on calling you and maybe coming down sometime soon; introduce you guys, ah...."

"Uh, hi." Ben came out of the bedroom, a hesitant smile on his lips as he gave a small wave. "I'm Ben."

His dad looked surprised, probably by Ben's stature and uniform. But surely they'd only have to look at the guy's handsome face, or that cute self-conscious smile, to see what a nice guy he was. Reece cleared his throat and introduced him.

"Ben, this is Marie and Allan. Mom, Dad, this is my boyfriend, Ben."

"Mr. Withers. Mrs. Withers." Ben put his hand out, shaking their hands. "It's nice to meet you."

Witness

Reece's father squared his shoulders and shook his hand. His mother practically glowed, shaking his hand and smiling up at him.

"Well." She turned to Reece's father, smiling, and then back to the both of them. "Aren't you handsome!"

Ben blinked and then laughed. Reece grinned at his mother.

"Um, thank you, Mrs. Withers."

"Oh," she said, waving her hand dismissively, "it's Marie." She touched her husband's stomach with the back of her hand. "Listen to him, so polite."

Reece laughed, looking at Ben apologetically. He motioned for them to sit. His mother and father sat on his loveseat, and he motioned for Ben to go ahead and sit in the only chair, then perched himself on the arm.

"So," his father began, his hands folded together between his knees. "Are you... actually an officer, Ben?"

The room was quiet for a moment before Reece started to laugh in embarrassment; Ben pressed his lips into a thin line. "Yes sir, I am. For a number of years now."

"Allan!" Marie hissed, looking mortified.

"What—oh." The man flushed red

Laughter filled the room, and the ice was broken.

"OH, WE have our thirty-fifth anniversary coming up. Ben you must come!"

His mother hadn't stopped smiling. Reece felt slightly foolish for thinking that introducing a boyfriend to his parents would have been awkward for them. His mother adored him on principle. She'd never had the opportunity to do the doting mother-in-law thing, and she clearly thought Ben was as lovely and gorgeous as Reece did. Not to mention that she had melted when she asked Ben about his own parents, and he'd told her about his father's death and that he'd never known his mother. Reece could tell she was aching to just hug the man.

His father had been a little slower getting comfortable. It was understandable, really; he'd never been in this situation before. And... well, the huge guy in uniform was screwing his son. But he'd seemed more than a little impressed when Reece had told them about the jumper incident, and that he'd even gotten on the news. Right now the two of them were talking about fishing, something to do with bait and rods. Reece wasn't following, but it warmed him to see genuine interest there.

"You'll have to come with Reece next time he visits"—his father looked him in the eye—"and he will come visit. I know a great fishing hole, the three of us will go down there."

Reece leaned against Ben's side and reached his arm around to rub Ben's shoulder. He knew that Ben would enjoy that—he hadn't been fishing since his father passed. He'd make sure to tell his dad how appreciated it was when they had a moment alone.

"I'd like that very much," Ben said, trying his best not to appear as choked up as he felt. He'd never done the "meet the folks" thing, and he'd had no idea what to expect. Reece's parents were exactly that—parents. They reminded him of his father, made him miss the old man, but feeling Reece leaning against him, rubbing his arm, he didn't feel the usual loneliness that would creep up when thinking of his father.

"Did Reece tell you about the last photo he sold?" Ben asked.

Marie's face lit right up. She hastily put down her cup of tea and touched her husband's arm. "Oh yes, the insurance thing? A beautiful picture, dear." She beamed at her son. "Your father even called the company to ask for 'information'," she said with a laugh, and Reece's father shifted uncomfortably. "They sent one of the leaflets, and Allan put it straight into his scrap book."

His dad was fucking adorable sometimes. For the past ten years he'd been so sure that there was this distance between them, that he'd somehow screwed up and pushed them away. Sitting there and listening as they chatted with Ben, he felt slightly ashamed for not giving them more credit.

"We keep everything he's had published," Marie continued. "We're so proud of you having your own business, sweetheart. Just like your father."

"I just make furniture," Allan insisted, "nothing like Reece, an artist traveling and taking pictures for magazines and books and what have you."

"Dad...." Reece shifted nervously. He could sense the confusion in Ben, but knew the man wouldn't refute anything his father was saying in front of him.

"Are you still planning on moving out, honey?"

"Um...." this was getting awkward.

"Last time we spoke, you said you were finally planning on moving into some place bigger, as soon as you had the time?"

"Well, moving takes a lot of planning and money...."

"But surely you can afford it now? Oh, you're just being lazy." She laughed, oblivious to Reece's discomfort and Ben's quiet confusion.

"Well, I'm just really busy right now, with shoots and the bike messenger gig."

"Oh, are you still helping out Darren? How is he, dear?"

"Darren's doing great. Jenny just got engaged." He attempted to change the subject away from work.

"Oh," she said softly, and Reece inwardly kicked himself at the sadness that was still evident in her voice after all these years.

"Ryan would be glad," his father commented.

Now Reece felt like shit. This visit needed to draw to a close.

"Who's Ryan?" Ben asked innocently.

His mother frowned and gave Reece a disapproving look. "He was Reece's brother, sweetheart. He and Jenny used to date. He passed away eleven years ago in an accident."

"Oh, I'm so sorry." Ben touched his knee in support, despite the fact that he hadn't been entirely truthful to him about his family, and Reece was grateful for it.

Perhaps sensing the suddenly awkward atmosphere, his father set his mug aside and stood. "We should perhaps be going; this was just a fly by visit. We're visiting with your aunt for a few days and just thought to drop by on the way."

Ben and Reece stood, and Reece hugged his mother and father. Ben shook his father's hand and smiled when Allan patted him on the shoulder as well. He laughed when Reece's mother insisted on hugging him and kissing his cheek.

"Make sure to come visit us soon!" she demanded. "The both of you."

"Sure thing, let me walk you down to your car."

Ben nodded to him, then waved again as they left the apartment. As soon as the door was closed behind them he let out a deep breath. That had gone great, but had left him a little anxious at the same time. Reece's parents, while nice and very welcoming, seemed to have a slightly rose-tinted impression of Reece's career. And the whole Ryan thing had definitely taken him by surprise, seeing as Reece had once told him he was an only child.

Outside by his father's car, Reece hugged and kissed his mother again.

"We'll call next time," his father said pointedly, and Reece laughed.

"Ben is wonderful, just wonderful." His mother beamed.

"Yeah, he is. Um...." he frowned as he picked his words carefully. "Thanks, for being so great. I—I always thought it might be a

Witness

little difficult for you—for me to introduce you to someone. With me being gay, I mean."

"And perhaps that was our fault," his mother replied softly. "We could have been a little more supportive. It just took us by surprise, and then with Ryan...."

Reece nodded quickly, not wanting to hear the words. "Compared to how you could have reacted I think you did okay. Especially considering what... what I did." His eyes began to sting.

"Hey." That was his father's firm voice. Reece looked up when a large hand rested on his shoulder. "We've told you about this. It was *not* your fault. When will you understand that?"

Reece swallowed the lump in his throat and nodded. His dad patted his shoulder again. "Anyway, we really should be going."

"Well, it was nice seeing you. And thanks again for being so nice to Ben."

"Of course, sweetheart," his mother said. She kissed him on the cheek, and then they got into the car and drove away. Reece felt slightly hesitant about going back up to his apartment, but he and Ben had been together for a couple of months now, and if Ben had any questions, he deserved to know the truth.

He walked back into his apartment to find Ben washing up the mugs they'd been using. "Hey," he said quietly.

Ben looked over his shoulder and smiled. "Hey," he replied, equally as quiet.

Reece took a deep breath and let it out in a little laugh. "Wow, so my parents love you."

Ben turned to face him. "Yeah? I'm glad. I was nervous." They were quiet for a moment, and then Ben put down the dishcloth he'd been using, walked over to where Reece stood, and pulled him into his arms.

Reece could tell Ben was waiting. Waiting for an explanation. Closing his eyes, he held onto Ben tightly for a moment before pulling back and diving right into it.

"I didn't mean to lie."

"To me, or to them?" There was no heat in Ben's words, but they still stung nonetheless.

Reece moved to sit on the couch, and Ben sat next to him. "Both," he replied quietly. "I exaggerated certain parts of my career to them. It's just an insecurity thing, ever since I came out to them."

"They didn't take it well?"

"They were alright; they just… became a little distant. Like they didn't know how to act around me anymore, you know?"

Ben nodded, though he didn't really know. "Well, they seem great with you now; I mean your dad has a scrap book of all your achievements, for God's sake." He grinned.

"I know, it's cute, right?" Reece smiled. "He's always done stuff like that. That's why I think it hurt a little when that stopped for a while, just a little while, when I told them I was gay. It wasn't malicious, it was just the unknown. Am I making sense?"

"Yes. But what does that have to do with you exaggerating your job?" Ben edged gently closer, his arm going around Reece's shoulders to pull him close so he could thread his fingers through the hair at the back of Reece's head.

"Well, I think I wanted to"—he frowned as he tried to find the right words—"I think I wanted to make up for being gay?" He knew the words were wrong as soon as he said them and shook his head. "No, I didn't mean that. I wanted to make up for the time I confused them, for the time they couldn't figure out who their son was anymore. We lost a good year as son and parents because of it." He swallowed. "And then Ryan…."

Ben nodded encouragingly. "Go ahead; I'm not mad. I'm not a dick and I can tell it's a painful subject."

"It's just that it was our second date and it's so hard to talk about. I'm sorry—"

"Whoa, hey, it's alright. I told you, I understand."

Reece gave him a shaky smile. "Anyway, Ryan—there was a car accident and he was killed. It was about a year after I came out to them, and I think the awkwardness between us just grew from there." He shrugged. "It was a hard time for us all; I had to get away and moved out soon after, when I was nineteen, to here. I missed them so much but I couldn't bring myself to be around them. It was just too difficult. I'm sure I made it feel like they'd lost two sons, but I think that it may have been worse if I'd stayed."

Ben nodded. "I can't imagine what you must have gone through, but I don't think you need to exaggerate to them. I know that's the first time I've met them, but I get the impression they'd be proud no matter what you did."

Reece nodded. "I think I'm starting to realize that."

Ben leaned close and kissed him gently. "You're a good guy."

Reece shook his head, not because he didn't believe Ben, but because he couldn't quite believe this guy was his. "Can we go to your place?"

Ben tilted his head. "Yeah, sure. How come?"

"I like your house." He shrugged. "I'm happy there. I want to be in your bed tonight."

Ben nodded and pulled them up. "Get your stuff together, feed your monster fish, and we'll go."

"Thank you."

Ben held his chin firmly for a moment. "Anything for you."

CHAPTER 8

REECE pulled his things out of the back of the cab and leaned through the window to pay the driver. When the cab pulled away, he gathered his belongings and made his way up to the porch of Ben's house.

He'd just gotten back from a shoot for a travel magazine—a shoot that actually required travel. It had been on the West Coast, in Los Angeles. It had been fantastic, and he'd gotten some good work done, but he'd cursed the timing.

He'd been recommended to the magazine by an agency he'd previously worked for. After attending a rushed meeting with his portfolio, they'd offered him the three-day job. Darren had given him the time off without a fuss, and Reece had been ecstatic. At least until he'd discovered that it required him being away on Ben's birthday. Originally, he'd intended to turn the job down, but Ben had insisted he go, and that they'd have dinner with Ted and Sharon as soon as he got back.

Now he was back. He'd only been gone a few days, but he'd missed Ben. It had surprised him to realize what a firm fixture Ben had become in his life. He'd called him, of course, to wish him happy birthday earlier that morning, and to promise he'd make it up to him, but he'd still felt like he'd dropped the ball in their relationship. It was the first birthday between them, and he didn't want this to set the tone for how things would be between them. Ben wouldn't come second to anything, and so he'd hauled ass out of there, rushed and gotten an

Witness

earlier flight out in time to be home—to Ben's house—before midnight on his birthday. He hadn't missed it.

He knocked and then let himself in. He dumped his suitcase in the hall and shucked his jacket. He picked up his larger side bag, the one he used for carrying his work in, and a shopping bag with the local supermarket's logo and name printed on it.

"Ben?"

He heard footsteps, and then Ben was there, a large grin splitting across his lips. Reece smiled at the delighted expression on Ben's face, and laughed as he was pulled into a bear hug. He only just managed to set the bags back down before dropping them.

"Hey," Ben said, laughing, "what are you doing here? I thought you weren't back until tomorrow."

"I couldn't miss your birthday, so I skipped out of there as soon as I could and got an earlier flight with"—he leaned back and looked at his watch—"twenty minutes of your birthday left!"

The sound of someone clearing their throat behind them drew Reece's attention to the person standing in the living room doorway.

"Oh, hey, Reece, I want you to meet Ted. Ted, this is Reece."

"Hi there, Reece." Ted limped over and held out his hand.

Reece smiled and took his hand firmly, "Hi Ted! It's so good to finally meet you, I'm sorry we had to cancel dinner tonight because of me."

Ted shrugged. "No problem, we'll still get together."

"I hope you don't have too bad of an impression of me for abandoning Ben on his birthday." He wound an arm around Ben's waist and smiled, but he really meant it. These people were Ben's family. He wanted to be liked.

"Nah, I think rushing home to surprise him probably makes up for that."

"Well, please apologize to Sharon for me, I can't wait to meet her too, unless… she's here?"

"No," Ben said. "Ted just came over for a beer and to watch a game. You'll meet her, though."

Ben couldn't have looked more pleased. Ted grinned and then cleared his throat. "Well I'm gonna head off, buddy." He patted Ben's shoulder and winked to him. "It was good to meet you, Reece; we'll get together with all of us soon."

"I look forward to it."

Ben saw Ted to his car. When he came back, he rushed up to Reece and pulled him into his arms. "You really didn't have to rush to get back, you know."

"I know. I wanted to, birthday boy." He stretched to kiss Ben again, smiling into it, just feeling happy as shit to be near him again. "I missed you."

Ben growled playfully, his hands straying to Reece's behind to squeeze. "Let's celebrate your return with birthday sex."

Reece laughed and pushed him back a little. "You bet, but first let's go into the kitchen; I've got a surprise for you!"

Ben raised his brow in question and grinned impishly. They headed into the kitchen, Reece taking his bags with him. "Sit yourself down on the stool and—" He spotted a large bouquet of flowers lying on the kitchen side, along with an envelope that had been opened and discarded next to them.

"You get flowers from work, or something?"

"Uh," Ben suddenly looked uncomfortable, "No, I was going to throw them out but got distracted when Ted showed up. They don't mean anything."

"Who are they from?"

Ben rubbed the back of his neck and spoke as nonchalantly as possible. "Jason."

Reece let out a disgusted little laugh before he could stop himself, and reached for the note in the wrapping of the bouquet. Reading it, he shook his head and then chucked it onto the counter. "He's sure got some balls." He wanted to act as if it didn't bothered him, but couldn't quite pull it off.

"Hey, come on, don't be pissed. You know it annoyed me, too, right?"

Reece didn't want this guy to ruin Ben's birthday, so he nodded his head. "What's with the envelope, a love letter?" He laughed without humor. Ben set his mouth into a hard line of disapproval, and Reece shrugged in apology.

"Something I'm sending back to him so he gets the point that I'm unavailable."

Reece nodded, then repeated his question. "So what *is* in the envelope? I'm just curious."

Ben sighed and looked uncomfortable. "Season tickets. Football season tickets."

Reece's eyes widened slightly. That had to have cost…what? Three, four grand minimum? *Fuck.* Either that dick really wanted Ben back, or he had no problem with splashing his cash around like some show-off asshole. He looked down at his bags, knowing that what he had gotten Ben didn't quite compare, and he felt embarrassed. Ben must have noticed, because his hand came under Reece's chin, lifting it.

"He is not coming between us tonight, or any other, for that matter. It's all going in the trash. The flowers and tickets, I don't want them, don't need them. "

"You don't have to do that on my account."

"Yes, I do. I'm your guy, remember?" The almost sad look in those blue eyes melted Reece, and he nodded, pulling Ben close for a gentle kiss.

Ben hummed into the kiss, then growled in annoyance when Reece suddenly pulled back and pointed to a stool. "Sit."

"What? No, c'mere." He grinned mischievously. "I haven't seen you in a couple of days; you're getting naked right now."

Reece snorted. "You can be such a brat." He shook his head. "Just a couple of days without sex and you forget all manners," he huffed disapprovingly as he pushed Ben against the counter and kissed him hungrily.

He pulled back, a little breathless, and wet his bottom lip. "I love that you want me, though." With that, he slid gracefully to his knees in front of Ben.

Ben groaned, his hands going straight for the tousled brown hair he loved so much to thread his fingers though. "Yes," he hissed, "missed you, Reece, missed that mouth."

Reece hummed appreciatively as he unbuckled Ben's belt and pulled his jeans and underwear down to his knees. He wetted his lip when the heavy cock he loved so much bobbed in front of him. He rubbed his hands up and down Ben's strong thighs, just nuzzling against his balls and pressing teasing little kisses against the base of his shaft.

"Please, honey, need you to suck me. Birthday boy, remember?"

Reece laughed. Taking Ben's cock in one hand, he looked the man directly in the eye as he licked over the head like it was a lollipop. Then he took the crown into his mouth and suckled, all the while staring up into Ben's lust-filled eyes.

"Oh fuck," Ben breathed, "you're going to kill me if you don't take me in your throat, baby."

Reece did just that, relaxing, steadily taking Ben down until his nose brushed into Ben's dark curls. He hummed and drew back, sucking hard. He kept doing it, swirling his tongue and sucking, up and down, his lips spread wide and moist around the hard cock in his mouth. Eventually Ben started panting and thrusting a little, his hands tightening in Reece's hair, guiding him up and down. Reece squeezed Ben's hips to let him know it was alright, and then Ben thrust hard a few times before erupting in his throat.

Reece swallowed every drop and then wiped his mouth. He pulled Ben's jeans back up as he stood. "Now, are you going to sit on the fucking stool?"

Ben laughed breathlessly and collapsed onto the stool, grabbing Reece's waist and pulling him against him. "Best present ever."

"Oh please," Reece said, smirking, hooking an arm around Ben's neck. "You get that present practically every day."

"The gift that keeps on giving," Ben said, leaning his brow against Reece's and kissing him lazily.

"You know, I did get you an actual gift."

Ben relented and let him go. "Alright, but good luck topping that heavenly blow job."

Reece grinned. "Close your eyes."

Ben laughed and shook his head, but closed his eyes nonetheless. He could hear some rustling, and then the sound of matches being struck. He grinned; matches on your birthday really only meant one thing.

"Okay, open them."

Ben opened his eyes and laughed affectionately. "Reece...."

On the table was a cake with candles already lit and ready to be blown out. There was also a bottle of wine, and a large rectangular gift wrapped in balloon-patterned paper with a bow attached. Just the two of them in the empty kitchen, no light save for the candles, and it was perfect. The perfect birthday surprise.

"I stopped by the twenty-four-hour store. It's not a real birthday cake and there aren't thirty-five candles, but I figure there's enough there to make a wish."

Ben didn't know what to say. No one had made a fuss over him like this for years. "Shall I?" He asked, pointing to the cake.

Reece nodded. "Make a wish."

Ben chuckled and did just that, then blew out the candles. Reece grinned and kissed him. "You don't have to eat any now, and the wine can go in the fridge, but everyone should blow candles out on their birthday."

Ben pulled Reece to him, letting him lean between his legs. "Thank you. You just made this a fantastic birthday."

Reece snorted. "Having your brains sucked out your dick will do that."

Ben laughed and rested his forehead against Reece's shoulder. "No one makes me laugh like you, you know that?"

"Yeah?" Reece asked softly. "Well, you make me as happy as a clown on crack. Now open your present so we can go to bed and fuck."

Ben snorted. "Such a romantic."

Reece winked and handed over the gift. It was pretty obvious what it was from the shape. "Is this a Reece Withers original?"

"It might be; open and find out."

Ben tore the paper, and his grin faded slightly in surprise and appreciation. "Reece…." It was a large, framed black and white photo of a stream with trees on either side, the sun shining through the leaves and silhouettes of a man and a small boy standing beside each other, fishing. The man had his arm around the boy's shoulders. Ben felt a lump form in his throat.

"I call it 'Father and Son'," Reece said quietly. He wrapped his arms around Ben's shoulders, and kissed his temple. "I want you think of fond memories every time you look at it."

"Thank you, Reece. I love it. I fucking love it."

"I'm glad. Flip it over."

Ben did so, and read the inscription that was engraved into the beautiful, lush, wooden frame.

Happy Birthday, Ben.

I love you.

Reece.

"And that's true, by the way." Reece said quietly, the corner of his mouth turning up in a hesitant smile. "I love you. Very much."

"Reece," Ben breathed, and pulled him close, holding him while he tried to get his emotions under control. When he was sure he wouldn't embarrass himself, he pulled back and kissed him gently.

"You know I love you too, right? So much." The kiss became desperate. "Love you so fucking much."

Reece smiled into the kiss; humming happily he wrapped his arms around Ben's shoulders and allowed the man to just take over. "Upstairs?"

Ben nodded.

Reece touched his chest as Ben reached for his hand. "You go on up and get into bed. I just need to grab something." Reece waited until he could hear the creak of the stairs as Ben made his way to bed before reaching into his bag for a few items. His pulse was still hammering. He'd said "I love you" before, but was only now coming to realize that he'd never really meant it, at least not like this. So he'd been hesitant about blurting it out too soon with Ben. There had certainly been opportunity enough where he could have happily let it slip out—

watching Ben cook, hearing him sing in the shower, watching him feed his weird cat… every time they went to bed.

He hadn't wanted to rush. He'd taken Darren's well-intentioned advice to heart, and felt that perhaps it hadn't been a bad idea to listen to him after all. Ben had certainly seemed happy to hear it, and he'd been surprised at the rush he'd felt, hearing those words returned. Just words. They were just words, and spoken by anyone else, he was sure they probably wouldn't have meant a thing to him. Glancing at the bouquet of flowers on the worktop, he smirked. Those flowers didn't mean a thing. Not to him, and more importantly, not to Ben.

He made his way up the stairs, unbuttoning the first few buttons of his shirt, with two large candles and a bottle of massage oil cradled in his arm. The door was left half open, and he smiled almost adoringly—he really was turning into a woman—at the man waiting patiently for him.

Ben was in bed, sitting up against the headboard, naked but for the sheets pulled up around his waist. Hearing Reece's approach, he turned his head to the door and put his palms down flat on the bed, sitting up straight. He looked expectant, and a crooked smile played across his lips.

"What have you got there?"

"These?" Reece raised an eyebrow, teasing. He placed the items on the nightstand and pulled his shirt up over his head. "Tools of seduction."

"Trust me, you don't need candles."

"I know. Usually all I need is you and a support for my back, and we're good to go."

Ben laughed. "Always so romantic."

"Ah, but that's what the candles are *for*."

Reece let his pants drop to the floor after fishing the matches out of his pocket, and walked to the night stand. He lit both candles and then turned off the lamp. The room became mostly dark but now had a warm glow to it. "See? you'll be putty in my perverted little hands now."

"Again, you don't need candles for that, but they are a nice touch."

Reece raised an eyebrow. "Say it...."

Ben rolled his eyes. "Fine," he said, laughing, "romantic."

Reece grinned and pulled the sheets back. "Heh heh, master of seduction," he muttered, but Ben heard and chuckled as he reached to pull Reece close.

Reece went willingly, growling playfully and pushing Ben onto his back. Ben smiled into the kiss. They both knew Ben could turn the tables anytime he wanted, but sometimes it was kind of cute to watch Reece get all assertive.

"You happen to notice what else is on the nightstand there?" Reece murmured against Ben's neck.

Ben craned his neck and raised an eyebrow in question. "Baby oil?"

"Massage oil." Reece kissed him, then grinned impishly. "For my baby."

Ben snorted. "Oh Christ."

"Shut up, I'm fucking adorable and you know it."

"Can't argue with that."

"That's better." Reece looked at the bedspread. "It might get a little messy, you mind?"

"I'm sure you'll make it worth my while... and you can do the laundry."

Reece sighed. "The price of being a stallion in bed."

Ben laughed, then quieted down when Reece narrowed his eyes playfully.

"Roll over, I'm going to rub you nice and slow."

Ben hummed and rolled onto his stomach, hugging a pillow under his chin. "You know, I've never had a massage before."

"Really?" Reece asked in surprise. "None of your past boyfriends…?"

"No, but then, I'm not sure if I'd call any of the guys I've been with serious boyfriends."

Reece settled himself astride the tops of Ben's thighs and poured oil over his hands, rubbing them together. "I've wanted to do this for a while now."

"Yeah?" He wasn't sure why he liked that.

"Oh yeah. A body like yours all slicked up? Hell yes."

"You do seem to have a thing for seeing me all wet."

"You wear it well," Reece said playfully. "And massage oil gives me a chance to be all grabbing on your ass without looking like I'm desperately trying to grope you."

Ben snorted. "I can't walk three paces in front of you without that happening."

Reece laughed and swatted Ben's ass. Then he set his palms on his lower back in a W shape and slowly rubbed upward. A low hum came from Ben.

"Don't fall asleep, got plans." Reece leaned forward, following his hands to Ben's shoulders, and stretched out along his back as he kissed Ben's neck. Reece grinned when he felt Ben undulate a little beneath him, rubbing himself against the sheets.

He sat up again, sliding his hands down the center of Ben's back, then around and up his sides and down his biceps. Ben had indeed turned to putty, much to his satisfaction. He looked amazing; the candle light flickered and cast shadows over his muscular, slick back. He'd hum every now and then. He sounded almost sleepy; he was so relaxed and blissed out. Reece loved how Ben's hips moved when his hands would skim teasingly over his lower back and that perfect behind. He leaned forward again, his hands on either side of Ben's hips as he murmured into Ben's ear.

"You still with me?"

Ben sighed and nodded his head, "Think I like this whole massage thing."

Reece smiled and kissed the back of his neck. "Was wondering if there was something else you might like...." He let his kisses trail down Ben's neck and between his shoulder blades. He moved his body lower in a graceful move that belied his unbearably aroused state, and let his tongue trail down to Ben's lower back.

"What—*oh.* Fuck yes." Ben raised his hips slightly.

Reece grinned, his hands skimming over those firm cheeks to gently part them. "I think he likes it."

His tongue slowly swiped over the tight hole and he grinned as a strong shudder wracked Ben's frame. With a groan, he repeated the action and then gently pushed in. His hands held Ben's cheeks greedily as he pushed in and out, a sensual indication of what was to come.

"Christ, Reece, please...."

With a groan Reece rocked back on to his heels before reaching for the nightstand and yanking it open with very little finesse. He ripped the condom open with his teeth, swiping his hands clean on the duvet before hurriedly rolling it on. He looked for wherever he'd put the lube, quickly stroked his rock hard dick, and then gently pressed into Ben with unsteady fingers. Christ on a stick, he was turned on. He lined up and slowly pushed into Ben's body at the man's urging, and groaned when he was completely surrounded by him. He rested his head between Ben's shoulder blades a moment, panting. When he felt Ben move his hips back, he steadily pulled out, then rocked back in.

"Shit, Ben...."

Following his instinct about what felt good, Ben rose to his knees and elbows, resting his brow on his forearms. Usually, he might feel vulnerable in such a position, being a bulky guy and all, but it felt damn good with Reece behind him. There was no room to feel self-conscious, just good. And the way Reece took a tight, dominating grip of his hips and rolled his own against him was nothing but erotic, pure and simple. He groaned as Reece leaned over him, his hands resting either side of him, letting his hips do the work.

"Reece...."

"God, look at you," Reece growled, rolling his hips faster. "Just giving it all up to me. Fucking beautiful."

Ben moaned deep in his throat, and reached for his bobbing cock. Reece moved his hand away, planting it firmly on the mattress, and then laid his own hands over his, entwining their fingers.

"Not yet, baby."

"I can't. Reece...."

His voice sounded desperate even to him. With a groan Reece pulled away, urging him onto his back, and hiked his thighs up and around his waist. "Gotta kiss you," Reece panted, pushing back in and closing in on Ben's lips at the same time.

They kissed messily as Reece began to move with harder, slightly more jarring thrusts. When they could no longer maintain the kiss, Reece buried his face into Ben's neck, murmuring to him as he began to fuck him more fiercely.

"Fucking love you, Ben," he panted in a husky voice. "Always gonna love you."

"Oh fuck...."

He wouldn't have been able to stop it if he'd tried. Ben's gut clenched and then he was coming, thick jets splashing hotly between them. Reece let out a guttural groan and thrust hard a few more times, his face still buried against Ben's neck. He shuddered, then stilled.

They stayed that way for a few minutes, just getting their breath back. Eventually Reece lifted his head and rested on one elbow as he ran his fingers through Ben's hair. "You okay?" he asked, kissing him softly. "Didn't go at you too rough or anything?"

Reece still lay on top of Ben, between his thighs, but it was oddly comfortable.

"No, was good," Ben murmured back, feeling sleepy.

Reece saw this and smiled. He kissed him tenderly. "Let's get cleaned up, then to sleep."

"Mm," Ben made a sound of agreement and then groaned as Reece slipped away from him.

Reece disappeared into the bathroom and returned with a warm, damp cloth that he wiped over Ben's stomach. Getting rid of the cloth, he quickly blew out the candles and climbed into bed next to Ben. With a quiet "C'mere," he pulled Ben close and tugged his head onto his chest. He kissed the top of Ben's head as he wrapped his arms around his broad shoulders.

"You asleep, birthday boy?"

Ben answered with an undistinguishable mumble.

Reece breathed in the scent of Ben's hair for a moment and then kissed his top of his head once more. "Love my cop," he whispered. Ben snored softly in reply.

REECE left Ben asleep in bed; he was rarely awake before Ben in the mornings, so he figured he'd take advantage of it. He cut two generous slices of cake to take up on a tray, as well as a small gift he'd forgotten about last night, but then decided to make a quick call first. He hadn't spoken to Darren in a couple of days, and wanted to thank him again for giving him the time off at such short notice, and perhaps to tell him briefly about the shoot. Of course, his friend didn't give a shit about any of that, and he grinned as Darren pelted him with questions over the phone.

"Tell me exactly what happened, who said it first?"

"You are such a fucking woman."

"No, I'm a gay man with an addiction to romance novels, now fucking *dish*."

Reece laughed. "I did."

"Yeah?" Darren's tone was gentle. "I was worried I might have freaked you out with that chat we had ages ago."

"You did!" Reece laughed again. "But I think it may have actually been good advice."

"Do I give any other kind?"

Reece ignored that. "I wanted to take it slow like you said, and when it came out, I wasn't waiting to be hurt—I didn't even realize I used to do that. It was just good."

"And what did he say?"

"Darren," he groaned, "for fuck sake. He said it back."

"So let me get this straight. You rushed back to surprise him, you brought him cake and wine and candlelight. You have what I'm assuming is amazing sex because you sound *way* too happy, and then you told him you loved him, and he said it back?"

"Not in that specific order, but… yeah." He couldn't help but smile.

"Why can't I meet someone like Ben? Or even you!"

"Well, gee, thanks."

"You know what I mean."

Reece smiled as he eyed the bouquet that had been left on the kitchen counter the night before. Darren chattered in his ear while he hunted for a vase. It didn't matter who sent them, it'd be a waste to throw them away. As for the envelope, he'd leave that for Ben to return.

"What are you doing? I hear rustling."

Reece paused. "Making breakfast," he said as he rearranged a few of the gardenias. "You'll find someone, Darren," he said softly.

"Oh fuck, listen to you."

"What?" He asked indignantly.

"I knew you were all smitten and shit, but fuck, you really do love this guy." The smirk in Darren's voice was obvious. And annoying. "Aw, come on, admit it—you feel like Cinderella, don't you?"

"No, Darren, I don't. And do you know why?"

"No, sugar, you tell me why."

"Because I'm a *man*. I've got a big fat one and I like to fuck other guys."

Darren was laughing over the phone now, and it made Reece grin. "And Ben isn't a prince, he's a cop. A big, sexy cop who fucks like a machine. He's a man. I'm a man. We're *men*." He nodded sharply. "Now fuck off. I'm arranging flowers."

He hit the end call button just as Darren began to laugh hysterically.

BEN awoke feeling relaxed and well rested. He stretched and lifted his head from the pillow, looking beside him at the space where Reece should have been. He rested his head back down when he heard the creak of the stairs, and smiled to himself. Well, well, well. Last night had really been something. He'd never really let himself go like that—had never allowed himself to be that vulnerable to another person. And it had been a real eye-opener.

He wasn't usually an enthusiastic bottom, but the connection he'd felt last night had been intense. Perhaps it had something to do with Reece telling him that he loved him, that he'd always love him. Ben grinned to himself. The words had been said in passion, but they'd been engraved into that wooden frame too. He'd never doubt them—or Reece—for a second.

"Hey, you."

Ben rolled onto his back and stretched his arms over his head. Reece sat on the edge of the bed beside Ben, a tray in his lap. Ben grinned and rolled onto his stomach again so that he could nose his head into Reece's lap.

"What you got there?" he muttered as Reece lifted the tray out of his reach with a laugh.

"Breakfast."

"Yum, what's for breakfast?" He pulled his head out of Reece's lap and sat up to look at the tray. He laughed. "Chocolate cake for breakfast?"

"Fuck yeah, birthday boy, remember?"

"That was yesterday."

"I'm taking into account that I was only there for the last twenty minutes of your actual birthday. You get an extended one this year."

"I like your logic. Gimme."

Reece snorted and handed over a bowl. Ben took the bowl with a grin and dug in. Then something on the tray caught his attention. "What's that?"

Reece gave him a crooked smile, and tilted his head to one side in slight embarrassment as he lifted the long-stemmed rose in clear wrapping and red ribbon from the tray. He cleared his throat and offered it to Ben, his big brown eyes gazing straight at him.

"Forgot to give it to you last night." He shrugged.

Ben took the rose, his brows lifted in surprise. A bemused chuckle escaped his lips. "You got me a rose. Reece Withers, you *are* a fucking romantic."

Reece actually looked away, a flush creeping up his neck, and Ben's chest tightened a little. Just when he thought this guy couldn't surprise him any more....

"I know it's not a bouquet or anything."

"It's better. It's personal. Fuck, I'm getting all misty-eyed because a guy gave me a flower." He laughed, and Reece chuckled along with him.

Reece cleared his throat and nodded at Ben's bowl. "Eat up."

Ben placed the rose on his nightstand and went back to his cake. "S'good."

"Yup. You realize that you're not exercising today, either, right?"

"I'm not?" Ben asked around a mouthful of cake.

"Nope, you're eating chocolate cake for breakfast, no exercise, and I figured since we both have the day free, we could go do something. Then in the evening we're going over to Ted and Sharon's for dinner."

Ben frowned and spoke around his mouthful. "They called? This early?"

"No. I called them." Reece looked slightly sheepish. "I used your phone to call Darren and thank him. Then I noticed that Ted was on your speed dial so I went ahead and made plans. I hope that's alright?"

"Yeah, it's fine." Ben reached out and stroked Reece's thigh, "I'm just surprised he picked up. He's not really an early riser—despite having two young daughters screaming over who gets to use the bathroom first thing in the morning."

Reece raised an eyebrow. "Ben, it's ten thirty."

Ben blinked. "It is?"

Reece nodded over to the clock radio. "Yep, you slept in for once." He smiled.

"Oh. Wow, I haven't done that in a long time."

Reece grinned mischievously. "Well, you did have an exhausting evening thanks to your stud boyfriend."

Ben laughed. Putting his bowl down, he lunged for Reece and pulled the man—who gave an undignified squawk—beneath him quickly, then pulled the bed sheets over both of their heads. Reece laughed, despite nearly being crushed by the larger man.

"So what did you have in mind for today, beautiful?"

Reece tilted his head to the side and smiled at that. "Well...." he drawled, "I thought that to begin with, we could get a little frisky in the bath."

"That's a given."

"Then...." Reece grinned boyishly. "How'd you feel about roller coasters?"

"What?" Ben laughed.

"Seattle may not have Disneyland, but we got a mean amusement park. Or how about the arcades? Plenty of those." He shrugged. "I thought we could relive our youth. Act like we were ten."

Ben just blinked for a few seconds and then pressed his face against the crook of Reece's neck as he started to laugh.

"What? You don't like them? We can do something else," Reece said.

"No, I like them, or I did when I was a kid. I haven't been to one since I was a teenager."

Reece grinned and touched the laughing man's face as he chuckled. "Then why are you laughing?"

Ben shook his head and then kissed Reece lazily. His voice was low and soft when he spoke. "I was just thinking earlier that you couldn't surprise me any more than you already do, then you go and say that."

Reece raised an eyebrow. "You can be pretty surprising yourself. Last night for example…."

Ben growled and pulled the sheets from over their heads. He groped along the nightstand for the massage oil. "That's something to put on the itinerary for today, I think," he murmured as he ducked his head to kiss along Reece's neck.

Reece closed his eyes and stretched his neck. "Oh yeah?"

"Yes. Though this time, I make you scream."

Reece groaned. "See? Always keeping me on my toes."

CHAPTER 9

HE WOULD not cry. He would not. Fucking. Cry. Bullies. Fucking teenage bullies. Making him look like a pansy ass. Reece told himself that the stinging in his eyes was not from the fact that two snot-nosed little fuckers had just knocked him off his bike and stolen it. It was from the split lip, the concussion, the probable broken ribs and twisted ankle, and… damn it, he'd loved that bike.

"Mr. Withers?"

Someone pulled the hospital curtain back, and when Reece first saw the uniform, he felt relief for a second, but that faded when he realized that it wasn't Ben. It was a younger guy. He looked nice enough, Reece guessed; he had his notebook ready and pulled the curtain back around to give them some privacy. But it wasn't Ben. He wasn't sure if that was a good thing or a bad thing.

"Yes?"

Nice guy offered him a small, sympathetic smile. "I'm Officer Brown; I'll be taking your statement."

"Okay, here it is." He made to shift himself into a more upright position but then thought better of it when his ribs began to scream. "Three huge, massive guys in their mid-thirties, with machetes and guns and—"

Officer Brown gave him a crooked smile and raised one eyebrow.

Witness

"Okay, fine. Two teenagers, probably around seventeen or eighteen. About the same height, six two, maybe. A hundred and fifty or sixty pounds. One looked a little heavier than the other. Um... one was wearing a ball cap, just plain blue, I think. The other had on a grey hoodie. I don't think I actually saw their faces." He shrugged. "But if anyone asks—"

"If anyone asks, they were huge guys with machetes. Got it." Officer Brown nodded, giving him a kind smile. "Can you tell me approximately what time this occurred, where you were, and what *exactly* happened?"

Reece sighed. "I was cycling through the park...."

"The one just south of—" Brown gestured over his shoulder.

"Yeah, I was going through the shaded part, between the trees and past the benches. No one else was around, but that's never really been a problem before."

Brown nodded. "Go on."

"I was on my bike—I'm a bike messenger—it was around five-thirty, my last delivery of the day." Reece paused. "Oh, shit, I think I left my backpack in the park. Those are confidential papers I was delivering."

"Don't worry about that now, we'll have someone swing by and look for you. Where did you first see them? Did they approach from behind?

Reece shook his head. "I didn't even see them coming. All I know is that I was riding along one moment, and then I was on the ground with my hands over my head, getting kicked in the stomach, the next."

Brown nodded as he jotted it down. "Did you see them as they ran away, hear them speak?"

"No. They laughed, and then one of them got on the bike while the other ran."

"And you took a blow to the head?" Brown gestured with his pen to the angry red and purple discolored skin around Reece's left temple and eye.

"Um." Reece cleared his throat. "No. When they were leaving, I tried to get up to run after them. I was kind of dazed, I think. I stepped funny and twisted my ankle, then fell and smacked my head on the path."

Brown nodded and jotted it down. "You know you have nothing to be embarrassed about, right? Taken by surprise like that, nobody would fare much better than you did."

"Thanks. Am I going to have to go down to the station or something?" Reece wasn't sure if he wanted to do that, or even what the protocol was for this kind of situation.

"No. We may need to speak to you again but you can head on home when the doctor gives you the all-clear."

"Just waiting for X-rays." Reece sighed. "I'm not going to see my bike again, am I?"

"We're going to do our best to get that back to you, but it's possible that you won't, no."

There was that stinging feeling again. "That bike was special. A gift, I mean."

Brown nodded sympathetically, and then a slow frown spread across his brow. He flipped back through the pages of his small notebook. "Reece Withers," he muttered, then glanced back at Reece. "You wouldn't know a Ben Jenkins, would you?"

Reece blinked in surprise. "Yes! He's my—uh...." He trailed off. He'd never asked Ben if his work colleagues knew he was gay. He knew Ben didn't hide it, but he didn't flaunt it, either, same as him. He didn't want to accidentally out Ben.

Fortunately, Officer Brown smiled knowingly and nodded his head. "You're Ben's Reece, aren't you?"

Well, that answered that question. Reece smiled softly. "Yeah, I'm his guy."

"I'm guessing he doesn't know about this, otherwise he'd be here. I'll give him a call for you." Brown reached for his cell but paused when he saw Reece wince. "I told you, you've got nothing to be embarrassed about. And Ben will kick my ass if he finds out I was the one who took your statement and didn't call him."

"Yeah, I suppose you're right."

"Don't you want him here?"

Reece pressed his lips together in a hard line. He would not fucking cry. "Yeah, actually, I really do."

BEN was furious when he'd pulled back that hospital curtain and seen Reece sitting there, all hunched over and bruised. The rage he'd felt when Brown had called moved to the back of his mind for the moment as concern and the overwhelming urge to comfort Reece took over.

Luckily the doctor had already been in to see Reece, and he was in the process of very slowly attempting to pull his sweater back on over his head. When Reece saw Ben appear, his brave front crumbled and his shoulders slumped. Ben walked right up to him, pulled the sweater away, and hugged him as gently as he knew how.

"You're okay," Ben whispered, unsure whether he was comforting Reece or himself.

Reece sighed and rested his cheek against Ben's shoulder. "Hi." He couldn't say anything more, the lump in his throat too thick, and too afraid that he'd embarrass himself if he tried. He lifted his arm gingerly to try and hold Ben close, and didn't even realize that a few tears had escaped until Ben was whispering to him, wiping them away.

"Hey, it's all right. You're okay. I've got you."

"Ah, shit," he said with a watery little laugh. "Just shock, you know? I'm not this much of a pansy ass I swear."

"You don't have to make excuses, Reece. Christ, look at you." Ben touched his thumb to his split lip, and gently kissed the bruised corner of his eye.

"Perhaps you should have been a doctor; that kiss feels better than the pitiful painkillers they gave me. I don't know who a guy's gotta blow to get some morphine around here."

"What did the doctor say, and what's that you're wearing?"

"Just a couple of bruised ribs, a sprained ankle and a slight concussion. I can go home, thank God." Reece looked down at the odd vest thing he wore that had hurt like a bitch to get on. "They said this was a pad. Kind of looks like a bullet proof vest, doesn't it?"

The pad was made of strong plastic with an absorbent material underneath. It did indeed look like a flak jacket—Ben had even worn something similar once or twice on the job. It hung on the shoulders and wrapped around Reece's rib cage, supporting him.

"Did you know you can actually buy these in sporting goods stores?"

"No," Ben murmured, frowning as he picked up Reece's sweater and rolled it up so Reece could slip his head through the neck hole. "Shouldn't someone have at least helped you get dressed?" There was a definite tinge of anger in his voice.

Reece pushed his head through the neck hole and winced as Ben helped him put his arms through the sleeves. "The nurse said she'd be back in a minute. I was supposed to wait for her, so no getting angry with the poor woman."

"I'm angry at the little bastards that did this to you."

Reece was surprised but oddly warmed by the conviction in Ben's voice. "That officer told you about it all, then?"

"Yeah, that was Brown. Good guy, we'll most likely be partners in a few weeks."

"Few weeks?"

"He's new and there's odd numbers in the department at the moment. We go with whoever needs company for the time being until Ted officially retires—which will be any day now. Paperwork and all that."

"Oh. He seems like a nice enough guy." Reece looked at him for a moment and then smiled softly—wincing a little when the cut on his lip pulled. "He asked if I was *your* Reece when I said the bike was special—that it was a gift. You been kissing and telling on me, Ben?"

Ben actually smiled. "No, I know Brown's okay about the gay thing, but I'm not sure how he'd deal with details. He just knows I've got someone important in my life called Reece."

"Someone important, huh?"

"Well, yeah, Reece. My heart goddamn stopped when Brown called and said you'd been attacked."

Reece had been teasing, but the sincerity and worry in Ben's voice touched him. He touched his cheek softly, and gave him a gentle kiss. "Will you take me back to your place?"

"Well you're definitely not going back to your apartment. Let's get you all signed out and we'll stop by your place to get a few things for the next couple of days. I don't think you could handle those stairs in your building just yet."

"Oh yeah, stairs. Kind of just wanted to be with you, but yeah, stairs are not my friend right now."

Ben touched his hand to the back of Reece's neck and kissed his forehead gently. "Brown's looking for your backpack. You can use my cell when we're out of here to call Darren or your folks if you want."

"I'll call Darren, just so he knows why the last package didn't get delivered and doesn't think I'm a total flake. I'll leave my parents be. It'll just freak them out."

The nurse appeared with a wheel chair, immediately frowning when she saw Reece was dressed. Reece pointed to Ben. "He helped me. I told him that I was supposed to wait for you but I couldn't stop him."

Ben rolled his eyes, and the nurse laughed. "He's rather charming, isn't he?" she said to Ben.

"I've always thought so. Come on, you, in the wheelchair."

REECE smiled as Roger left the apartment building in a hurry and headed over to Ben's cruiser. He hit the down button for the electric window and smiled reassuringly at the old guy. He looked close to tears, bless his heart.

"Hey, Rog."

"Reece! Ben told me you were attacked. Was it a hate crime?" He leaned down to look through the window. Ben was leaving the building just behind, a duffel bag in hand.

"I'm okay, Rog, just some bruised ribs and a twisted ankle. I need to take it easy for a few days. And no, they just wanted my bike."

Honestly, between Roger, Ben, and Darren, the warm and fuzzies were going to kill him. Darren had begun to rip him a new one over the phone until he'd managed to get a word in and explain what had happened. That only made things worse; the guy had practically burst into hysterics, and not the laughing kind. It'd taken Reece a little while to convince him he was okay, but he'd finally calmed Darren down when he'd explained that he was with Ben and being looked after. Not before having to give him Ben's address so that he could come over the next day to see him, that is. He was sure Ben wouldn't mind.

Ben dropped a hand on Roger's shoulder. "Don't worry, Roger, I'll look after him. Why don't I drop by in a few days so you can come over and visit? We can play poker, have a guy's night."

"That sounds like fun," Reece added, just loving Ben all over at that moment.

"Well, if I'm not imposing?" Roger looked hopefully between them.

Reece could tell the guy was delighted at the thought, but trying to tone it down—not wanting to be inappropriate. Reece smiled. "Of course not, we're buds, aren't we?"

Ben dropped the duffel in the back of the car and then leaned against the rear door, giving them a moment. The cell in Reece's hand began to ring and he handed it out of the window to Ben. Ben walked away a few paces to speak quietly to the caller.

"Yes, Reece, of course." The old guy's eyes began to mist over, and then they lit up with an idea. "And maybe I could feed your fish for you until you get back?"

"That'd be great, Rog, thanks a million."

Ben came back then, ending the call and smiling at them both. "We've got your backpack."

"That's so great, thanks, Ben."

Ben shrugged. "Brown found it. He's heading over to my place now to drop it off, so we'd better take off." Ben smiled at Roger kindly. "How's Monday sound for poker?"

"Oh, wonderful! I'll bring some beer."

Ben laughed and was about to tell Roger that he was sure he'd have some in his fridge, but a glance at Reece told him to indulge him. "I'll pick you up at around seven if that's alright."

"I'll be ready. And Reece," he said, leaning back down to look through the window, "you let Ben look after you like you did for me, you hear?"

"I will." He ignored Ben's curious look for the moment and patted Roger's hand. "You take care and we'll see you soon."

"Soon, yes." He straightened and then pointed a finger at Reece before heading back inside. "And make sure you give your parents a call, just to let them know where you are and how you're doing."

Ben had climbed back into the car and started the engine. Reece promised that he would call his parents, and they both watched to make sure Roger made it back inside alright before pulling away.

"Did you call Darren?"

"Yeah, and I hope you don't mind, but I gave him your address. He said he'd come by tomorrow to make sure I'm alright. I don't think he believed me."

"Yeah? Great. It'll be nice to finally meet him."

"Won't you be at work?"

Ben frowned and glanced over at him. "No, of course not. Like I'd leave you alone when you're hurt."

"Ben, I've got a headache and sore ribs."

"And a sprained ankle. You heard that nurse, no weight on that foot for a few days."

"Then why did they give me crutches?"

"The crutches are for you to use in a few days time when it's healed a little. Even then you need to take it easy for a while."

"You won't get in trouble at work or anything?" He felt like a nuisance.

"No, it's fine. I've got a pretty good attendance record; they'll understand. I'll just give you a hand with things for a few days until I know you can get about okay without me."

"Thanks."

"Hey," Ben said softly, "what's with the sad face? You know I don't mind looking after you, right? You're mine to look after."

Reece felt a little heat touch his cheeks at that. Freakin' cute. "I know. I just… feel like a bit of a nuisance." He shrugged self-consciously. "You always take care of me; I feel kind of… I don't know, selfish?"

"What are you on about?"

"Just little, considerate things. Little things that I adore you for, but that I sometimes wish I could return."

"How'd you mean?"

"Well, like how you always cook for us. Or like when I'm paying for a meal, you'll pick something less expensive?" He gave Ben a crooked smile to let him know that he didn't mind those things, just that he was aware of them. "Or like how you drive us everywhere whenever we go out. You're so fucking considerate like that. I wish I could even it out a little, do stuff like that for you."

"You have no idea what it is you do for me." Ben said in a serious tone. Reece was about to shrug it off out of embarrassment, but Ben wouldn't let him.

"No, I mean it. Take my birthday; I don't think I've ever felt that loved by someone who I wasn't related to. You rushing back from an important shoot? That gift? You knew what that picture would mean to me."

That picture now hung in his living room above the fireplace, above the photos of his family. It was one of the most wonderful gifts he'd ever received. He could tell Reece was fighting back his emotions, so he reached over and rested his hand on his thigh. The poor guy had had quite an evening.

"Do I need to keep going until you turn beetroot?" he teased, and Reece laughed.

"No, I'm good." He swallowed and then spoke quietly. "Love you."

Ben squeezed his thigh. "Love you." He pretended not to notice Reece quickly wipe his cheek and turn to look out of the passenger window, and squeezed his thigh again before putting his hand back on the wheel. "And you know, I could always teach you to drive."

It hit him like a physical blow. It always did. Reece forced out a small laugh, glad that they were now pulling up to Ben's house, where a second cruiser was parked, so that he wouldn't have to say anything further on the matter.

"There's Brown."

Reece stayed put—he didn't really have much of a choice—as Ben went to speak with Brown. He kept it brief, taking the backpack and clapping the guy on the back. To Reece's confusion, both men walked over to where he sat patiently.

"Okay, let's get you in and settled."

Reece didn't quite understand what he meant until Ben unfolded the wheelchair from the back of the car. He groaned, and both cops grinned. "Come on, it's a sprained ankle, I can hop up the porch."

"You want to hop up the porch with bruised ribs and a concussion?"

Shit.

"That's what I thought," Ben said smugly, earning himself a glare. Ben leaned close to him and spoke quietly. "Just let us get you up the porch in this thing, then Brown'll take it back to the hospital, and you won't have to see it again."

"Fine."

He'd only been in the car for a half-hour tops, but his body had already completely stiffened up. He was embarrassed to have to let Ben help him out of his car seat, especially seeing as he'd managed to get into it okay on his own. Embarrassment gave way to amusement however, as the two burly cops struggled to get his ass up the porch in the chair.

He was relieved to be seated on Ben's couch, and even more relieved to see that chair disappear. Ben went to make coffee as he shifted about, trying to find a comfortable position.

"What do you want for supper, handsome?" Ben called.

"I'm not sure if I have much of an appetite." Reece squinted over at the fireplace where the framed photos of Ben's family sat, and smiled at seeing the new addition.

"You really should have something in your stomach after those painkillers you took."

Reece looked up as Ben came back into the room, carrying two mugs. Reece smiled his thanks as he took his mug and blew over the surface. "Thanks."

"No problem. So, supper. I can throw something together, or we can order in. Something greasy and comforting."

"You know what I'd *really* like?" Reece gave him his sweetest, most pleading look.

"I don't think you're up for that," Ben murmured as he ran his fingers through the hair at the back of Reece's head.

"No, not that, though—fuck, that's going to be annoying." He closed his eyes as Ben did that thing with his hair that always had him purring like a kitten.

"What? No sex?"

Reece actually whimpered and nodded. "I'm just a little bruised; hopefully it won't be for long. So no looking hot in the meantime."

"I'll make sure to stop showering, brushing my teeth and hair and...."

"That won't help. Love your bed head, it's so cute." He chuckled.

Ben smiled in surprise. "You kidding? I look like Muddles first thing in the morning."

Reece laughed loudly and nodded. "That's what's so cute!" He groaned a moment later and touched his side. "Ouch."

"Poor baby." Ben laughed affectionately and kissed him softly, just under his jaw. "Tell me what it is you *really* want, then, and I'll see what I can do."

Reece bit his lip. "Pie?"

"You want some pie?" Ben shrugged. "Might have a frozen one we could—"

"No I... your pie, the one you bake sometimes, with the blueberries?"

A warm smile slowly spread across Ben's lips. "You want me to bake you a pie?" Those big brown eyes just gazed up at him. Ben groaned. "As if I could say no to those peepers. Let me see if we've got the ingredients."

Reece grinned triumphantly and called after Ben when he went into the kitchen. "You're awesome!"

"Damn straight I'm awesome," he called back as he searched the fridge. "Either that or you've got me extremely well trained."

"A bit of both, I think."

Ben closed the fridge and leaned his head back around the corner to glare at Reece. Reece gave him his best shit-eating grin and winked as he took another sip of his coffee. Ben shook his head and laughed quietly.

"You've got me wrapped around your little finger, haven't you? You little shit."

He heard Reece bark a surprise laugh in the living room, then call back to him: "Can wrap you around something else, if you like."

Ben groaned and shook his head. He should really know better by now that Reece, being the complete smartass that he was, would always get the last word in. And it would more than likely be funny as hell.

Reece was damn near giggling when Ben walked into the room. Ben grinned and put his hands on his hips. For some reason this sent Reece into a fit of laughter, making him clutch at his sore sides as he groaned.

"Stop laughing!" That would have gone over so much better if Ben hadn't been laughing himself. "You'll hurt yourself."

"Ah, Christ, sorry," he tittered. "Just, you were glaring and looking all big and sexy and shit, then you put your hands on your hips and you… you—" He started giggling again, "you looked like my mom!"

Ben groaned. "You're impossible!"

"Oh, God, this hurts!" Reece said, still laughing.

Ben rolled his eyes and then walked over to the couch and leaned down to shut the man up. He kissed Reece hungrily and then pulled back suddenly, taking pride in the owlish, dazed look on the injured man's face. "Now shut the fuck up."

Reece smiled lazily. "'Kay."

Ben sat beside him, and put his arm around Reece's shoulders. "How badly do you want pie?"

"Kind of want something more now…." Reece leered and let his hand wander into Ben's lap. Ben caught the hand with a disapproving look that was ruined by his snort of laughter when Reece pouted.

"I don't have all the ingredients, so I can either nip out and get them, or we can order something in. Up to you."

"Oh. Then don't worry about it, you've been at work all day and shouldn't have to go back out. Let's get pizza."

Ben stared at him for a moment and then let his head thump against the back of the couch with a groan. "I'll go get changed and head out to the store. Anything else you want?"

Reece beamed at him, "You're so good to me. Can we have ice cream too?"

Ben smiled and took Reece's face in his hands to kiss. He fucking loved this guy. "Vanilla?"

"Yeah." Reece grabbed Ben's sleeve as he made to stand up. "Wait! Um… cookie dough ice cream?"

"You want cookie dough ice cream with blueberry pie?"

"Yeah, don't worry if that's too weird for you. Just give me the tub and I'll burrow for all the dough and you can have the vanilla."

"Generous of you."

"I try."

"Anything else?"

Reece shook his head no, then grabbed for Ben's sleeve again. "Oh! Um, marshmallows? And some pretzels?"

Ben straightened and raised an eyebrow. "Christ, I've knocked you up."

"Ha ha."

Ben winked and gave him a quick kiss on the cheek. "I'm going to get changed. Then I'll be gone twenty minutes, tops. Try not to hurt yourself in the mean time."

"I'll try." Reece managed to swat Ben's ass as he walked by. "Cheeky shit."

Ben grinned and handed Reece the remote to the TV. "Watch some television, and stay put."

Reece saluted him.

BEN had been quick about getting the pie ingredients, not to mention the marshmallows and pretzels. He shook his head and grinned as he locked his car. Stupid little shit like that just made Reece all the more loveable to him. He opened his front door and went straight to the living room, stopping short when he found it empty.

"Ben?"

Ben was startled to find Reece sitting on the stairs, looking rather sheepish. Ben dumped the bags and climbed the stairs two at a time to kneel in front of him. "Did you fall? Are you okay?"

"Yeah, sorry, I—"

"Why the hell did you get off the couch? *How* did you?"

"The crutches," Reece said defensively. He chewed on his lip guiltily. "I think they're down there somewhere. I dropped them."

"What are you doing on the stairs?"

Reece shrugged, looking embarrassed. "I needed to go to the bathroom; you don't have one downstairs so…."

Ben groaned, and Reece flushed a little. "I'm sorry, I should have waited, but I thought I could do it. Turns out you were right about the whole waiting to use the crutches thing." He fiddled with the material of his pants. "I am a nuisance," he said quietly.

Ben touched his cheek gently. "No. You're not. You're just going to have to rely on me for a few days. Just for a couple of days, then you should be able to get about alright by yourself."

Reece nodded and offered him a shy smile. "You couldn't help me up the rest of the way, could you?"

"I don't know how you made it this far, to be honest." Ben helped Reece to his feet slowly, and frowned as he tried to figure out how to help him up the remaining stairs without touching his sides or letting Reece's sprained ankle touch the floor.

"You don't know how badly I have to pee," Reece said, laughing weakly. "I was worried you were never going to get back. I was into my fourth rendition of 'Halfway Down the Stairs' when you came in."

Ben frowned, still trying to adjust his hold on Reece. "You were reciting poetry?"

"Huh?"

"Isn't that a poem by A.A. Milne?"

"Um, I have no idea, I was singing the song."

"Song?"

"Yeah, you know?" Ben shook his head, and Reece rolled his eyes before singing the first few lines.

"*Halfway down the stairs is a stair where I sit. There isn't any other stair quite like it. I'm not at the bottom; I'm not at the top; so this is the stair where I always stop.*"

Ben stared for a moment before snorting and laughing. Reece narrowed his eyes and glared. "You're just jealous of my mad singing *skills*."

"You can't sing for shit, but you're definitely cute as hell." Ben shook his head, and then he sighed. "Okay, this is no good; I'm going to have to carry you."

"What? You are *not* carrying me."

"I can carry you or you can get carpet burn shuffling up on your ass. Now stop being awkward and hold still."

"Ben! I'm not some damsel in distress and you're not Superman." He slapped away Ben's hand, and Ben glared at him.

"Oh for fuck's sake, just let me help you!"

"I'm not an invalid!"

"No. You've got a sprained ankle and bruised ribs. Now I can leave you stranded here, or you can let me help you."

Reece flushed sheepishly, "You're sure I'm not too heavy? You won't drop me?"

"Baby, I bench press more than you every day. And I won't drop you, I promise."

Reece sighed. "Well in that case, get a move on, Lois Lane needs to piss pronto."

Ben laughed, and as gently as possible, lifted Reece into his arms. Reece hissed, and Ben winced in sympathy. "Put your arms around my neck."

"Oh, Christ, I am a woman."

"Shut up," Ben huffed as he shifted Reece into his arms. He knew that the arm he had around Reece's back couldn't be comfortable, and quickly adjusted his hold under Reece's legs so he wouldn't drop him.

"How's the rest of that song go?" he asked, hoping to take Reece's mind off of any pain he was in.

"You want to hear it?"

"Yeah, it's kind of sweet." Ben grinned as Reece hid his face in his neck with an embarrassed sigh and quietly sang the rest.

"Halfway up the stairs isn't up, and isn't down. It isn't in the nursery, it isn't in the town; and all sorts of funny thoughts run round my head; it isn't really anywhere, it's somewhere else instead."

Ben put Reece down on his feet and then took him by the face and kissed him tenderly. "You're fucking adorable, you know that?"

"I swear you just said butch and hung, and not adorable."

Ben laughed, and patted his ass in the direction of the bathroom. "I'll wait here."

"Surely going downstairs would be easier than going up?" Reece called.

"I don't care, I'm carrying you. Now piss."

"Sir, yes sir!"

Ben shook his head and waited a few moments. "So who turned the poem into a song?"

There was a pause, and then the sound of the toilet flushing before Reece appeared in front of him. "You're kidding, right?"

Ben shrugged. "I've only heard the poem."

"Fucking intellectual. Robin sang it. Ring any bells?"

"Robin, as in...?" He looked down the stairs, "Okay maybe I don't have to carry you down, if you can get an arm around my shoulder or middle without it hurting too much."

"Thank God. And *Robin*. As in Kermit's nephew?" Reece put an arm gingerly over Ben's shoulder. It actually hurt like a bitch, but he really didn't want to be carried again. They began to slowly descend the stairs, Ben lifting him gently to save him putting weight on his foot.

"Kermit?"

"Are you fucking serious?" Reece laughed, then winced. "Kermit *the Frog*."

"You mean like the Muppets, 'Sesame Street'?"

"Oh, finally, he sees the light," Reece said. "Can I sit in the kitchen with you while you cook?"

Ben smiled and helped Reece into the kitchen, then went back to grab the shopping bags. "Think the ice cream may have melted a bit."

"Put it in the freezer, but pass the pretzels here." He held out his hands and licked his lips.

"So you like the Muppets, huh?" Ben grinned at him as he rolled up his sleeves and set out the ingredients on the counter.

"Hell yeah. Who doesn't?"

Ben turned around and lifted his hands up. "Can't say I do. But then I *am* thirty-five."

"Yeah, and I'm twenty nine, what's your point?"

Ben snorted at the pissy tone of voice. "I'm not going near that one."

Reece shook his head and spoke around a mouthful of pretzel: "No, you would love them; you just need to be educated."

"I'll have to take your word on that."

"Nope, I am *so* making you watch *Muppet Treasure Island*. Oh! And *The Muppet Christmas Carol*."

"Christ, I've opened Pandora's box."

"Come on, how can you not love the Muppets?"

"Quite easily, actually."

"Miss Piggy? With her karate chops? Elmo, Grover, Aloysius Snuffleupagus...."

"That's the elephant, right?"

Reece shook his head. "No, woolly mammoth. Then there's Oscar the Grouch, Telly Monster, Cookie Monster, The Count, *Bert and Ernie*?"

"Baby, you saying weird names isn't going to make me suddenly understand your odd fixation."

"Every gay man should be familiar with Bert and Ernie."

"And why is that?"

Reece rolled his eyes, smiling. "Everyone knows that they're lovers."

Ben stopped what he was doing and looked at the man incredulously. "Okay, Reece, seriously, can you hear yourself?"

"They are!" Reece said. "They live together, share a bedroom; I'm telling you the sexual tension is very palpable." Ben raised an eyebrow and said nothing. Reece cleared his throat. "You're going to break up with me now, aren't you?"

Ben laughed and reached over to give Reece a quick kiss. He couldn't stop with the kisses tonight; perhaps what happened to Reece shook him up more than he originally thought. "No. As weird as you are, I still like you."

"Good to know."

"Which was the one that didn't talk on *Sesame Street*? It was a scientist and had orange hair."

"That's Beaker, assistant to Dr. Bunsen Honeydew. And he was part of the Muppets."

"Isn't it the same thing?"

Reece shook his head smugly. "There's always been this misconception that the Muppets and *Sesame Street* are the same thing. They're not. Although Kermit does make guest appearances on *Sesame Street*."

Ben shook his head. "How do you know all this shit?"

Reece shrugged. "I loved it as a kid."

"So who's your favorite?"

"That's a toughie. I think I might have to say Swedish Chef."

"Do I want to know?" Ben asked, laughing.

"He's the only human-like Muppet. He cooks ridiculous food and sings in mock Swedish." Reece laughed. "He starts to cook and sing and I *completely* lose my shit."

Ben laughed. "Okay, I might have to see that. Just so that I can see you giggling your ass off."

"You won't be sorry!" Reece promised.

During the weirdest conversation Ben had ever had, he'd finished the pie, and was now putting it in the oven. "Okay, you little weirdo, let's go into the other room while that cooks."

They got seated comfortably, and Reece immediately pulled Ben closer. "C'mere, I wanna make out."

"Let's put on a movie or something." Ben grinned. "I don't have any Muppets, but how about a little more Hitchcock?"

"Sounds good. You know, if they ever made a Muppet version of *Psycho*, I'd be in heaven."

Ben split a side laughing, popped in the film, and then went back to the couch so that they could make out like teenagers.

BEN smiled as Reece finished his second helping of pie and ice cream. Reece really could pack it away. Lord knew where it all went—there wasn't an ounce of fat on him. Ben put his bowl on the coffee table, and did likewise with Reece's once it was empty. The movie was finishing, and they sat more or less cuddled up. He let his hands run lazily through Reece's hair, the man's head resting on his shoulder.

"You alright? Not in too much pain?"

"I'm fine, kind of sleepy, actually."

"Why don't we make it an early night? You've had a terrible day, and we've got Darren coming over tomorrow. Want you awake, don't we?"

"Mm, alright. I'll try my best to keep my hands away from you tonight, but I make no promises."

"It won't be too difficult, seeing as we're not sleeping in the same bed."

Reece's head shot up. "What are you on about?"

"You know I always pull you to me in my sleep. If I did that tonight it might hurt you."

"I don't want to sleep in a separate bed. We're not some married straight couple!"

Ben let that one go and began to sit up. "One night won't kill us. I'll sleep in the guest room right next door. If you need anything you can just call, or throw something at the wall."

"Ben, come on," Reece groaned, "I was kidding, I promise I won't try to start anything."

"Just tonight, Reece. I'm not budging, so stop pouting."

"I don't pout," he said, pouting.

Ben smiled affectionately and kissed him briefly. "Let's get you upstairs."

Reece groaned and allowed Ben to help him up. "Fine, just tonight, though."

Ben got him to the bottom of the stairs; Reece was holding his crutches, claiming that if he needed to use the bathroom in the night he would get there his damn self. Ben decided not to push him on that one. You could only test a man's patience and pride so far. They both sighed when they got to the bottom of the stairs.

"You got down okay, so let's see if you can get up with my help but without me carrying you." Ben would give him that, at least.

Witness

Making their way up the stairs was slow business. Ben got the feeling that Reece wanted to change his mind and be carried, but he knew the man's pride wouldn't let him ask.

"You doing okay? I can—"

"Nope, this is fine."

Ben said no more about it. "Can I ask you something?"

"'Course you can."

"Earlier tonight, when Roger said for you to let me take care of you, like you did for him, what did he mean?"

"Oh, that. I told you he lost his wife a couple of years ago, didn't I?"

"Yeah, you mentioned it."

"Well, the poor guy was devastated. He loved his wife, they were married for more than fifty years, and she was a real nice lady too. I looked after him for a couple of weeks, just made sure he was okay," he said, shrugging, "you know."

Ben frowned. "How do you mean?"

Reece shrugged again, playing it off as casual. "I stayed with him, the guy would…." Reece looked at Ben seriously. "Don't let on you know any of this to Roger, okay?"

"Naturally."

"Well, he would wake up crying. I mean, he was a real mess, Ben. It was heartbreaking. I slept on his couch for a couple of weeks, so he wouldn't be alone. Made sure he got up and dressed every day, made him some lunch, took him to the doctors." Reece sighed and said, "Just kept him company. He doesn't have any other family."

They were in the bedroom by then, and Ben was dumbfounded. "You did all that, for an old guy who lost his wife?" His voice was barely there.

"It's Roger," Reece answered, sitting on the side of the bed gingerly. As if that explained it all. "He's kept an eye out for me ever since I first moved into his building when I was nineteen."

He carefully helped Reece get undressed and climb beneath the sheets. He sat on the edge of the bed as Reece got comfortable among the pillows, and reached out to brush the hair from his forehead.

"You're a good guy, Reece," said quietly. "My father would have loved you."

Reece smiled in surprise. "Yeah? I wish I could have met him."

"Me too."

"I saw the new addition above the fireplace, by the way." Reece murmured, turning his head to nuzzle into Ben's hand.

Above the fireplace, there was a series of framed photographs: photo's of Ben's mother, of his father, of him with Ted and Sharon and their kids. Mostly they were of Ben and his father. But there was one new photo there, of him and Ben.

After Ben's birthday, Reece had met Ted and Sharon by going over to their place for dinner one night. They'd gotten along really well, and he'd had a great time. He'd also offered to take a couple of photos of their kids when Sharon had expressed an interest. They'd chosen a date and they'd had fun during the small shoot. He'd refused to take payment and the photos were now back at his place, ready to be delivered. But at one point during the afternoon, Sharon had taken his camera and ordered him and Ben to stand together. He'd looked shyly at Ben, and Ben had pulled him right into his arms, making him—and the kids—laugh.

It was a great picture. The lighting wasn't perfect, neither was the stance or setting. But Ben was looking at him with amusement and affection, and he was laughing right down into the lens. Ben had asked for a copy of the picture, and Reece had given it to him without a second thought. But it meant a lot to him that it sat framed next to Ben's family photos.

"I love that picture."

"I like where you put it," Reece said quietly.

"I've put it exactly where it belongs, with the rest of my family."

Reece couldn't really think of anything to say, but it didn't matter. Ben leaned down, and kissed him softly.

"'Night, baby, I'm right in the next room."

Reece nodded, and as Ben sat up, he reached out and took the man's hand, stopping him for a minute, and brought it to his lips to press a kiss against his knuckles. Ben smiled softly, and Reece let the hand go.

REECE tried to be as quiet as possible as he hobbled into the guest room on one crutch. Ben was asleep, looking as gorgeous as ever. The covers were twisted around his waist and he slept with one arm slung above his head. His black hair was already a mess, and Reece smiled at the sight. His plan to just slink beneath the covers next to Ben proved futile as he landed half on top of the man, startling him awake.

"What—Reece?"

"Oops," he whispered sheepishly.

"Are you alright? You need some painkillers or...."

"I'm sorry; I didn't mean to wake you."

Ben frowned. "What are you doing up?"

"Couldn't sleep." As he spoke he moved the sheets back and edged into the bed beside Ben. Ben unconsciously moved back to give him space, then groaned, realizing what he was doing.

"Reece, I thought we discussed this?"

"Give me a hand?"

Ben begrudgingly helped Reece lay back, and pulled the covers back over both of them. Reece grinned. "I don't remember the last time I slept in a single bed. I've certainly never shared one."

"This is ridiculous, we're both crammed into a single when there's a perfectly good double next door."

"I like it, being all squished up next to you. You can't get away from me now."

"Reece," Ben groaned. "I don't want to hurt you."

"You couldn't in a single; we're too close together to bump each other. Now hush."

Ben sighed, and they took a few minutes to get comfortable. Eventually Ben lay behind Reece, spooning him but trying not to touch him. Reece growled in frustration when attempting to reach for Ben's arm to pull it around him.

"Ben," he said in all seriousness. "I was attacked today. I just want—*need* to be near you, okay?"

The room was quiet for a moment, then Ben shifted closer, just enough that their bodies lightly touched. Reece reached back with a wince and yanked Ben's arm back around him.

"Fucking cuddle me."

Ben sighed, and then he gently pulled Reece flush against him. He brought both arms around him and held him close. "Better?"

"Much, thank you."

Ben kissed the side of his neck. "Go to sleep."

CHAPTER 10

REECE sighed as he watched Ben put on his uniform. He'd been at Ben's house for about a week and a half. He no longer had to wear the pad around his midsection, and his sprained ankle was more or less healed. However, he did have to use his crutches for another week, and he still found it difficult to put his shoes on. The subject of when he might be going home came up only once, and Ben had put an end to that discussion by stating that the stairs in his apartment block were not ideal for a guy on crutches. Reece wasn't about to argue with that, though he was starting to get frustrated.

He missed being active. He could get around the house just fine but that was about his limit. Despite that, even if he could ride his bike (if they ever found it) or be fit enough to climb his own stairs, he wasn't sure he wanted to, and he was worried that Ben had started to notice. He wasn't about to let two teenage delinquents turn him into a hermit, but he'd never been attacked before, not even punched. And right now he felt safe in this house; he wasn't quite ready to leave it yet. Luckily, doctor's orders prevented him from having to confront those feelings.

"Maybe you could give Darren a call, you guys could hang out?"

Reece smiled. He knew Ben felt guilty leaving him alone all day, but the guy had to work, and he didn't need a baby sitter.

"Nah, he's got work stuff."

Ben sighed and buckled his belt with a frustrated, jerky motion. "How about Roger?"

"Ben, he's elderly and I'm not exactly mobile at the minute. I'll be fine on my own; I have been for the past few days."

Both Roger and Darren had been over to visit. They'd had a nice time with Roger; he'd brought the beer and a *pound cake*, for some reason. They weren't sure why, but it was sweet of him all the same. Darren and Ben had gotten on like a dream; it had been creepy but nice to know that the two people he loved most had become fast friends. They'd been lucky in that respect, he and Ben. He found it difficult to see how anyone couldn't like Ben, or Darren, for that matter, but he knew it wasn't always the case with best friends and boyfriends. On this occasion he'd lucked out, and the two of them had even swapped numbers.

"I don't like leaving you by yourself. What is there for you to do?"

Reece sat up a little against the pillows. His legs fell open and the duvet bunched around his waist. "Well, I can watch TV, nap, or snoop through your stuff." Reece grinned. "I should warn you, I'm not tired and I'm getting bored of television. Heh heh."

Ben smiled, but it was half-hearted. "You want me to go by your place after work, pick up a few more things?"

Reece bit the corner of his lip. "You don't mind? I could use some more clothes, not that I don't love wearing yours, but I kind of look like a kid wearing his dad's stuff."

Ben grinned and said, "I like how you look in my clothes."

"I'll do some laundry today."

"You don't have to—"

"Ben. I can do laundry." He watched his hands as they spread over the bed sheets. "And I have to do something; you've been looking after me and doing everything for me—"

"So?" Ben shrugged, sitting edge of the bed and strapping on his watch. "You'd do exactly the same for me."

Witness

"Yes, I would, and I'm glad you know that, but even the doctor said to start moving about and to steadily put a little weight on my ankle. That's why when you get ho—back later; you'll be coming back to a cooked meal!" Reece said, beaming.

Ben raised an eyebrow. He'd caught the inflection and hadn't minded one bit. Reece's cooking was another matter. "You know Hot Pockets don't count as a cooked meal, right?"

"Actually, I was thinking along the lines of spaghetti and meatballs, smartass. It looks easy enough to cook and you have the ingredients already. What do you think?"

Ben couldn't help but chuckle at Reece's eagerness. "Sounds good to me, just don't burn down the kitchen."

Reece glared playfully. "Your faith in me is touching."

"I'm sure it will be wonderful." Ben leaned down and kissed him, then stood and headed toward the door of the bedroom, where he hesitated. "You know, after we eat, how about we go see a movie or something, maybe go have a beer?"

"Um, we could, or you could pick one up from my place and we can make out on the couch."

Ben tilted his head to the side, frowning slightly. His voice was soft as he said, "Reece…."

Reece looked down at his lap and shrugged. When he looked back at Ben, his expression was hard. "I'm just not in the mood today."

Ben sighed, sensing that they wouldn't get anywhere with it this morning without him upsetting Reece, so he let it drop. For now. "I should get going."

"Wait…." Reece made to reach out his hand but then dropped it to the bedspread; he hadn't meant to sound so ungrateful. "You don't have to go yet, do you?"

Ben shrugged. He didn't have to, but he didn't feel like arguing with Reece, either. Technically they never had argued, and he didn't want to start now, or at least not when he'd have to leave Reece all alone straight after to go to work.

"I'm sorry, it came out wrong."

"We're going to talk about this, Reece; you can't let those two little...." Ben trailed off and sighed when Reece's cheeks flushed with what he assumed was embarrassment. He walked back over to the bed and lifted Reece's chin gently. "You've nothing to be embarrassed about."

Reece pulled away from Ben's touch with a sharp movement, his already heated cheeks turning red. "I know that!"

"Then what's the problem?" Ben's voice rose right back.

Reece winced and blinked at the tinge of anger in Ben's voice, and found that he didn't know how to answer. Instead he looked down at his lap and fiddled with the edge of the duvet. His brows drew together and he clenched his jaw tight. He could only shrug.

Ben's shoulders slumped and he felt a stab of guilt at the dejected expression on Reece's face. "I'm sorry. I guess I'm still angry at what happened to you. Not you."

Reece nodded, and Ben did likewise. "Make sure you're careful going down the stairs, I'll be back a little later tonight. I'll call...."

Reece reached out and pulled Ben to him, taking him by surprise. Ben had to dart out a hand to catch himself so he didn't land on Reece, and frowned as Reece pressed their lips together. "Reece...." he pulled back.

"Just kiss me." Reece asked, sadness creeping into his voice. "Please?" Without waiting for an answer, he reached up to try and kiss him again, but Ben pulled back.

"Baby," he said softly, "it's okay." He wasn't sure what he meant by that, but the need to reassure Reece was there. He'd never seen him that vulnerable before, not even in the hospital.

He pressed his lips to Reece's brow, and felt him sigh. He touched Reece's cheek. "I gotta go." He felt Reece's hands grip the front of his shirt.

"Fuck me first."

"Reece," Ben groaned.

"I'm fine now, just tender. Come on, Ben...." He pushed the duvet down with his legs, leaving him naked, and gave a hesitant smile. His smile wavered a little when Ben took his hands in his own and gently extracted them from his shirt.

"We shouldn't," he said gently, knowing that his actions confused Reece. "I'd be furious with myself if—"

"Since when did I have to beg you?" Reece gave a little laugh, though it was painfully false. His voice sounded small and hurt. "Don't you want to?"

Ben stared down at him, torn. He groaned and then knelt on the bed, one knee on either side of Reece's legs as he fumbled with his belt, trying to unbuckle it. Reece's hands replaced his as he pulled his shirt from his pants and unbuttoned it as quickly as he could. Reece's hands pushed the shirt off of his shoulders, and Ben dipped his head to crush his lips to Reece's.

"How could you ever say that? Huh?" Ben gasped between kisses. He pushed his pants down his thighs and gently laid his body over Reece's, using his hands to hold most of his weight off of him. "You have no idea how hard it's been, not touching you, not fucking you...."

"I wasn't sure... didn't know what to think."

"Don't you ever doubt me."

"I won't. I'm sorry. Please...."

With Reece's help, he shucked the rest of his clothes and reached toward the nightstand. He prepared Reece as cursorily as he dared, and lifted Reece's thighs up and around his waist. "You tell me if it starts to hurt anywhere, I mean it."

Reece nodded and bucked his hips up, trying to push against the blunt head of Ben's dick. Ben rested his brow against Reece's and pushed in slowly, his mouth falling open and his eyes closing in pleasure. He gritted his teeth and growled deep in his throat. Reece was already panting and grabbing desperately at Ben's shoulders.

"Need you."

Ben rose up on his arms, moving his hips slowly to begin with. Reece tried to pull him down against him, but Ben shook his head firmly. "No, will *not* hurt you."

Reece nodded, his hands landing on Ben's hips, urging him to pick up the pace. Ben complied but wouldn't pound into him like he knew Reece wanted. His hands gripped tightly, bunching in the sheets on either side of Reece's shoulders as his hips rolled in more and more exaggerated movements, making Reece whimper.

"Fuck," Ben moaned, "I love it when you whimper like that. All helpless and needing me."

"Oh God...."

Ben leaned on his elbows so that one hand could rest on the top of Reece's head, holding him as his thrusts became sharper, deeper. His other hand roamed along Reece's hip and thigh, hiking it up his waist. He slowly began to fuck him in earnest, but always holding back that little bit that usually roared between them.

"Love you, love you, Ben...."

He took Reece's mouth hungrily, pulling away only when it became too difficult to maintain a rhythm and kiss him at the same time. Tears leaked from the corner of Reece's tightly closed eyes, and he kissed them away. "Shh, I'm here," he soothed.

"Ben." Reece's plea was so desperate, so needy that it triggered something within Ben, and his orgasm rapidly began to approach.

Witness

"Come for me, come all over us," Ben grunted, and allowed a few sharp jarring thrusts to send him over. He heard Reece cry out, and felt warmth spread between them. He kept moving, going slowly and just riding it out. Ben didn't allow himself to collapse on top of Reece, but stayed where he was, buried deep inside of him. His breathing was steadily returning to normal, his head resting against Reece's neck. He spoke quietly to him, earnestly.

"Whatever insecurities you were thinking about us before this, you forget them, you hear me?"

He felt Reece nod, and he lifted his head to look into those big, blissed-out brown eyes. "I love you too."

HE WOULD not laugh. He would not. Fucking. Laugh. He had come home to pandemonium. As soon as he'd stepped through the door, Reece had come hobbling out of the kitchen on a crutch, banging into the small table in the hallway as he went, to stop him from going any further. He'd held his hands up in defense, and had been ordered upstairs to change while Reece dished up supper. Now he sat opposite Reece as the man served congealed spaghetti and what he assumed were meatballs. Either meatballs or small lumps of charcoal, he wasn't sure.

"Um, I'll clean up all this up after we eat. I was hoping to do it before you got home, but time kind of ran away from me."

"Uh huh," Ben said, grinning. The kitchen no longer looked like his kitchen. It looked as if Reece had used every single pot and pan he owned; it was an absolute mess. Strangely enough though, he liked it. It felt cozy, like a home should.

"Well," Reece said as he rubbed his hands together excitedly—God the man was cute sometimes—and gestured for Ben to go ahead and eat. "Dig in!"

Ben cleared his throat to cover the laugh that was bubbling up in his throat, and picked up his knife and fork. He looked up just as he was about to take a mouthful to see Reece watching him expectantly. He forced himself to not grimace at the odd taste, and swallowed while making a yummy noise. He couldn't help but grin a little as Reece's eyes narrowed slightly in suspicion—the guy knew his expressions too well by now for him to fake something convincingly.

The chef tried some himself, and Ben watched in amusement as Reece shifted in his chair and coughed a little to hide a grimace himself. "Tastes a little different from your spaghetti and meatballs."

Ben shrugged, feeling sorry for him but dying to laugh at the same time. "Different isn't bad."

They ate in silence for a few more minutes before Reece put his knife and fork down with a clang. "Seriously. How the fuck did I screw up spaghetti and meatballs?!"

Ben couldn't help but snort and reached for a napkin to cover his mouth as his shoulders began to shake with silent laughter. Ben looked up, ready to apologize, but just laughed out loud at the self-deprecating smile on Reece's face. He sat back and shook his head as he tried to get his chortling under control, and watched as Reece stood gingerly and reached for the phone. Reece sat back down and dialed, looking at Ben as he put the receiver to his ear.

"Yeah, hi, can I get two mediums with spicy beef and pepperoni, green peppers and extra mushrooms?"

Ben just about fell in love with the guy again when Reece, after giving the address, smiled and winked at him. He admired that in a person—being able to laugh at your own embarrassment. Reece put down the phone, and they looked at each other quietly for a moment, just grinning.

"I should never cook," Reece announced.

Ben nodded his head.

"I did everything the packet said to."

"And yet...." Ben edged, smiling and wincing sympathetically.

"And yet it tasted like shit. Why did the spaghetti mush and clump together like that?"

"I think you may have over cooked it a little."

Reece nodded. "I'm guessing that would be the cause of death for the meatballs also?"

Ben pressed his lips together to keep from laughing and nodded. Reece laughed, and then stood. "You go and take a load off, I'm going to start cleaning this up."

"I'll help." Ben took the two plates from the table, but Reece waved him off and snatched the plates away.

"You've been at work. Go get settled, I won't be long." He forked the food into the trash can that opened up under the sink. "I guess it should have clued me in when I couldn't get Muddles to eat one of the meatballs."

Ben didn't reply, but came up behind Reece and wrapped his arms around his middle. Reece turned his head to the side and gave him a handsome smile as he filled the sink with water. Ben kissed the crook of his neck. "I love that you tried."

"At least I didn't fuck up the laundry, I—" Reece trailed off as his words reached his own ears.

"What?" Ben asked when Reece stopped mid-sentence.

Reece laughed and shook his head. "You remember when I told you that you'd make a great housewife some day?"

Ben frowned and then laughed as he remembered. "The irony."

"I think you'd better do the cooking, and I'll stick to the laundry from now on—for as long as I'm here, I mean."

Ben gave him a gentle squeeze, rubbed his stomach, and kissed his cheek. "Sounds good to me."

Reece gestured toward the living room with his head. "Go relax and keep an ear out for the door, this won't take me long."

Ben patted Reece's ass and did as he was told. "You're too good to me."

"Not really, you're paying for the pizza."

BEN had never seen anything so hysterical in all his life. Before coming home, he had stopped by Reece's place to pick up some more clothes for him. He'd also picked up a couple of his books and DVDs so that he wouldn't be so bored all day when Ben was at work. Right now Reece was collapsed against him, pizza forgotten, crying—literally crying—with laughter as Swedish Chef attempted to make chocolate mousse with an actual moose.

He had to admit, perhaps the Muppets were amusing, but even more funny was Reece laughing like a lunatic. Reece rolled onto his front and pressed his face into Ben's stomach. Ben laughed loudly and ran his fingers through Reece's hair as the man's shoulders shook uncontrollably. He reached for the remote and turned the TV off.

"I'm turning this off before you give yourself a hernia!"

Reece didn't move, and Ben doubted that he could have even if he'd wanted to. He lay between his legs, gripping Ben's sides, keeping his face hidden against his stomach, while laughing like a two-year-old.

"Baby!" Ben laughed. "You weren't kidding about losing your shit, were you?"

Reece just shook his head against his stomach, and Ben leaned over to cradle the man's head to him and kiss that wavy brown hair. "Seriously," he said, chucking, "you're freaking me out a little here."

Reece managed to get himself under control, only snorting and chuckling a little every so often. He propped his chin on his hands to look up at Ben, but otherwise didn't move. He sighed. "I love the Muppets."

"You don't say."

"Thanks for bringing it over, and the other stuff."

Ben shrugged, smiling down at him. "No problem."

Reece looked up at him, a mischievous grin spreading across his lips, then lifted himself on his hands to press his lips against Ben's. Ben hummed into the kiss, letting Reece take control of it, groaning when he felt a hand cup him through his jeans. Reece's lips left his and his T-shirt was being pushed up his chest, not removed but pushed up to his neck as Reece kissed his chest and then took a nipple into his mouth and sucked.

"You have *the* most beautiful body," Reece groaned, licking along his abs.

Ben arched beneath him and gave a breathless laugh as Reece kissed along the waistband of his pants. "You're teasing."

"That's 'cuz I love it when you get all squirmy."

Ben arched again, groaning as Reece scraped his teeth against the bulge in his jeans. Reece popped the top button open, but then looked Ben right in the eye as he gripped his hips and pulled down the zipper with his teeth.

"Oh Christ, this is gonna be quick."

Reese's grin was sinful as he pulled the jeans down Ben's hips in one tug. "Love it when you don't wear underwear," Reece said huskily, as Ben's cock lay flat and hard against his stomach. Ben looked incredible. He was already panting lightly, flushed along his neck, with his shirt still pushed up and his jeans around his thighs. "*So* fuckable," Reece groaned.

Reece sat up for a second to push Ben's jeans down past his knees so that he could spread his thighs properly. He rubbed his hands up and down Ben's thighs and nuzzled against his balls. "Love going down on you."

Ben groaned and pushed his hips up. "Never had it so good, I swear."

Reece chuckled. "Haven't even started yet."

"Not what I meant, but don't let me keep you."

Reece knew what he meant, he knew because he felt the same. He'd never been as happy as when he was with Ben. And it wasn't just the sex, it was everything. He made everything good. Ben's quiet plea from above brought his attention back, and taking Ben's dick in hand, he wasted no time in swallowing him down whole. He was going to make him scream.

"Fuck!"

Reece's head began to bob over his cock, and Ben could only watch and grip his shoulders and the back of his head as the tension built with record breaking speed. "Oh shit…."

Reece was taking him all the way down and sucking hard on the slide up, swirling his tongue around his head before filling his throat again. Ben could feel his hips lift off of the couch as he began to thrust, and groaned when Reece tapped at his entrance with his thumb, just pushing the tip inside. It was enough to make him thrust up hard with a shout, and come deep in his throat.

Reece let Ben slip from his mouth and then eased his jeans back up his legs with a satisfied smirk. He lay on top of Ben as the man fought to catch his breath, and lazily kissed along his jaw.

"I swear you're trying to kill me," Ben groaned.

"No. But what a way to go…."

Ben laughed and stretched his neck with a contented sigh as Reece kissed along his neck. "You're spoiling me."

"Not nearly enough," Reece whispered as he reached to nibble on Ben's earlobe. "How about we go upstairs?" he murmured, and slowly thrust his hips against Ben. "I want you. Want to have you again and again, all night."

"Shit." Ben laughed breathlessly. "Let's go. Now." He urged Reece up, who climbed off of him and grinned smugly.

He found Reece's crutches and handed them to him. He knew Reece hated using them, especially as his ankle had mostly healed up, but doctor's orders were doctor's orders. "These things must make me look *so* sexy," Reece joked as he made his way to the stairs with Ben behind him. They looked at each other when the phone rang.

"I'll get that, be careful going up."

Reece slowly made his way up the stairs and then stripped off his clothes in the bedroom. He was tempted to pose naked in the center of the bed to make Ben laugh, but decided that he didn't want Ben laughing, he wanted him moaning. He sat on the edge of the bed, leaning back on his hands as he looked down at his midsection. The bruising was light brown and the green unflattering color all bruises turned before disappearing. To be honest, he wasn't sure what Ben saw in him at the moment, he was a mess, but he wasn't going to rock the boat.

He grinned as Ben came into the bedroom. "Hey, Gorgeous, you've got ten seconds to get naked."

Ben grinned and pulled his T-shirt over his head. "Or what?"

"Or I come over there and rip your clothes off with my teeth."

Ben raised an eyebrow and unzipped his jeans. "Yes, sir."

Reece laughed. "Who was on the phone?" He gestured with his head for Ben to get his ass on the bed.

"Sharon. She wanted to see how you were doing."

"Oh yeah? That was nice of her."

"I would have given you the phone, but you know how she can talk. I said you were napping."

"Lying to your friends, Ben? Shame on you."

Ben lay back and let his legs drift apart as Reece rested on top of him. He tilted his head back and closed his eyes as those amazing kisses trailed down his neck again. "Well, if I had given you the phone, I never would have gotten laid tonight."

"Good point. Feel free to lie on my behalf any time."

"She, uh, she also invited us over tomorrow night."

Reece lifted his head to look Ben in the eye. He'd seen Ted and Sharon and his own friends over the past couple of weeks, but they had come to him. He hadn't actually left the house since he'd been hurt. Logically he knew it was foolish to just pretend the rest of the world didn't exist, and that he could just stay with Ben always, but he still felt ridiculously hesitant about leaving.

"What did you tell her?" he asked quietly.

"I told her I'd call her back when you were awake. That you might not be feeling up to it." He tilted his head to one side and cupped Reece's cheek; his brows drawn together in worry. "Reece...."

"Tell her we'd love to."

A relieved smiled spread across Ben's face. "Yeah?"

Reece sighed and nodded, then gave Ben a shaky smile. "I know," he said quietly, those two words conveying to Ben that he was aware of how he'd been—that he knew he was worrying him. "I could do with the fresh air." His hand touched the back of the one that cupped his cheek, and he kissed Ben's palm. "I'm sorry for worrying you. I'll be better."

Ben shook his head and reached up to kiss him. "You know it's understandable, right? You know I get it?"

Reece nodded his head, "I know you do, and not just because you're a cop. You understand because you get me."

Reece leaned on his elbow and ran his fingers through Ben's black hair. His voice was low and seductive. "You know, I was planning on fucking you raw, but now I want to make love to you.

Love you with everything I got." He took Ben's mouth with a deep, slow kiss, and did just that.

"SO HOW'S he really doing?" Ted asked.

Ben leaned against the kitchen counter and watched as Reece leaned down, one arm curved protectively around his ribs as he rubbed Chicken's belly. Sharon sat beside him with a coffee mug in hand, laughing at whatever he was saying.

"If you had asked me that yesterday," Ben answered quietly, "I would have said 'not good'."

Ted closed the refrigerator and uncapped his beer, leaning against the counter beside Ben. "And now?" He took a long pull from the bottle.

Ben nodded his head, proud of Reece. "He's facing it. He was avoiding leaving the house, tonight's the first...."

Ted's brows rose. "Really?"

Ben nodded his head. He knew Ted would be the guy to talk to about this. He understood it; he was a cop. *Former* cop. He wouldn't look at Reece weird or badger him about it. He wouldn't mention it at all.

"He chose to come here; I didn't nag at him. That means he's doing better, right?"

Ted hooked his arm around Ben's neck. "I think he'll be just fine, just go slow with him. Coming over to our house and going out aren't exactly the same, but he's no coward; he'll be fine when he's ready. Just be there with him when he is."

Ben nodded, and looked up when Reece called him. He and Ted went over into the living room and sat down. Ben leaned back against the couch, his right heel resting on his left knee and his arm draped behind Reece's shoulders. He took a swig of his beer and stretched his neck forward when Reece gestured to whisper in his ear. He smiled and set his beer down on the coffee table and stood up.

"I'll be right back."

"Where's he off to?" Sharon asked.

Reece grinned. "We made a quick stop on our way over here." They'd stopped by his apartment to say a quick hi to Roger, and so that Ben could go up and get the photos of Tracey and Amy that were developed and ready. He'd wanted to make a nice gesture for Sharon and Ted, who he knew were very special to Ben, so he'd had three of the photos framed in dark mahogany. They hadn't been cheap, but he'd always loved spending money on gifts.

Ben came back in with his large carry folder, and Sharon immediately clued in and clapped her hands. "The photos are ready?"

Ben grinned and set the folder down, unzipping it. He hadn't seen the pictures yet, and was as intrigued as Sharon and Ted. The kids were sleeping over at a friend's house tonight, but he knew they were eager to see them too. He let out a soft "Wow" as he lifted them out and handed them over.

There were the three framed by Reece, and then the other copies on boards covered in clear protective plastic. Reece really was an amazing photographer. One picture had the two girls sitting back to back on one stool, dressed alike and grinning at the camera. Another had them hugging each other tightly, their cheeks pressed together. Amy was laughing her girly little laugh, her eyes sparkling, and Tracey had the most adorable look of indulgence on her face as she grinned cheekily at the camera. As if she was asking the viewer to humor her sister.

The final photo was a family photo. Since the shoot had taken place at their house, all four of them had been there. Initially Sharon had asked for just photos of the kids, but at the last moment Reece had put them together in one shot. It had been a good idea. Sharon had Amy in her lap, and Ted had Tracey in his. They sat huddled together; the girls were holding hands and laughing. Ben couldn't remember what joke Reece had told to make the girls laugh, but it had certainly tickled them. Ted and Sharon just grinned away as their girls laughed; it was a picture of a happy family.

Sharon covered her mouth with her hand and gasped. Ted leaned forward to take one and his face lit up with a smile. He put his arm around Sharon and set it in his lap. "Aw, Reece, now these are great, really great. Aren't they, Sharon?"

Ted looked at his wife and then laughed. She was waving one hand at her eyes that had teared up and held a framed photo in her other. "Let me see," she said, leaning over. She looked at the one Ted held and let out a watery little laugh as a tear slipped down her cheek.

"Now don't be daft, woman," Ted said as he laughed and kissed her temple.

"They're beautiful, just beautiful, Reece. Come here, you."

She stood and took Reece's face with both hands and kissed him smack bam on the lips. Reece's look of surprise had both Ben and Ted laughing. Sharon wound her arms around Reece's shoulders and hugged him tightly. Reece chuckled and hugged her in return, patting her back affectionately.

"You know, that's the first time I've ever been kissed by a girl." Reece laughed.

"Oh Christ," Ted said, watching his wife wipe lipstick off Reece's mouth with her thumb. "There's no getting away now, buddy."

"What do you mean?" Reece asked.

"She's given you the seal of approval. You're family now."

Reece gave a hesitant smile and glanced at Ben; for some reason he couldn't help but flush a little when Ben winked at him. Ben glanced at Ted, nodding his head in thanks.

"Let me go get my checkbook." Sharon said, sniffing.

"Hey, now, I told you, no charge." Reece stopped her.

"But those frames alone—" she started to say.

Reece waved her away. "Kids as cute as yours? They needed to be framed, and I knew where I could get some that would match great with your furniture. So don't worry about it, they're a gift."

Sharon looked at Ben. "Oh, you are definitely keeping him."

Ben pulled Reece to sit back down beside him, his arm finding its way around his shoulders again, bringing him close. "That was the plan." He felt warmth spread through him as Reece leaned against him comfortably, and rested his hand on his thigh as if it were the most natural thing in the world.

"Well, then," Sharon said softly, looking oddly satisfied at the two of them sitting together, "if you won't take our money, then I'm sending you home with enough leftovers to keep you boys going for weeks."

"Now that I'll accept," Reece said with a grin

"When my girlfriends see these, Reece...." She was holding one of the frames again, admiring it. "They are *all* going to want your number. Do you have some business cards I can take?"

"Not on me, no."

"Just tell them to call the house if they want to get a hold of him," Ben offered.

"I'll do just that." Sharon said with a happy nod of her head.

"Well," Reece interrupted apprehensively, "I might not be able to work right away; I'm still a little tender."

Ben shot Ted a look, but the guy gave nothing away. Reece's hand played with the fabric of Ben's jeans for a moment before he cleared his throat and spoke brightly. "But then I can always take future bookings. I should be fine in a week or so."

Ben squeezed his shoulder. He was proud of him. He looked back at Ted, and this time Ted smiled and gave him the smallest of nods. Ben knew then that Reece would be fine.

Witness

"I CAN'T believe you're making me do this." Reece moaned.

"Come on, you've been inactive for too long. A run will do you good."

Ben had convinced him—with the promise of on-demand blow jobs—to go for a jog. He was now fully healed, not even a little achy. And he'd left the house a few times with Ben, just to do little things like going to the store, and even once to go swimming to loosen up his muscles (they knew now that it was not a good idea, as Reece had liked the sight of Ben in his swim shorts a little *too* much). He felt no trepidation about going out now, in fact, if he were honest, he felt a little foolish for having let it bothered him at all.

"I guess. I'm worried that my fitness has gone to shit."

He'd been at Ben's for nearly a month, just taking it easy and getting back on his feet. If he never saw another pair of crutches again it would be too soon. But now he was due back at work, *both* works. Thanks to Sharon he had a couple of bookings coming up. And thanks to Ben, he was due back to work for Darren. He still couldn't believe it. Ben had come home with a surprise not two days ago; he'd bought him another bike.

The two kids had been found, but had already sold his old bike. While he was relieved to know he wouldn't be running into them again, he'd been pissed about losing *another* bicycle. Enter Officer Wonderful.

He'd been speechless, touched, and grateful, but a little overwhelmed. Ben had done so much for him in the five months that they'd been together. He'd bought Reece two bikes, and taken him in and looked after him when he couldn't take care of himself. He adored the man. *Loved* him. But he felt like he had taken a little too much from Ben. He felt as if he, himself, was not enough to repay all that Ben had given and done for him. Of course he had said none of this to Ben, because he knew Ben would have none of it. He'd accepted the bike with gratitude, but had made Ben promise that it would be his birthday gift to him.

"Argh, I hate running!" He was embarrassed to find himself becoming a little breathless already. Ben, of course, looked like an athlete.

"You're bound to be a little winded to begin with. Just get into a rhythm, and tell me if you want to rest."

Reece did just that, keeping stride beside Ben and breathing as evenly as he could. Eventually it started to feel good. He hadn't even realized how much he'd missed the burn of muscles as they were stretched and used. If he could jog, he was pretty sure he'd be fine working tomorrow. All the same, Darren had reassured him that he'd take it easy on him, and not give him too many drops.

"Let's walk for a bit." Ben put his hands on his hips and ambled along. Reece wanted to collapse on the ground in relief, but slowed to a walk instead, tipping his head forward and stretching his arms behind his head.

"You're not doing too badly for someone who doesn't run."

Reece could hear the teasing note in Ben's voice and grinned. "Let me sit your ass on a bike for eight hours and see how well you do then!"

Ben laughed, then quickly licked his lower lip and looked a little unsure as he glanced over Reece's shoulder. "Do you want to go through the park? We can go through, then head back home," he said softly.

Reece's smile faded, and he looked over his shoulder behind him. He had no idea Ben had led them this way. In fact, it had never dawned on him how close the park he'd been attacked in was to Ben's house, though they had been jogging for a while. He felt slightly betrayed when he looked back at Ben. This must have been obvious because Ben came over to him, one hand going to his arm and the other gently touching his face.

"Hey, I'll be right there with you."

Reece shook his head. "You couldn't have given me a little warning? You had to spring it on me like this?" he asked in a quiet voice.

Ben looked remorseful. "I didn't think you'd come if I did." He pulled Reece into his arms, and, begrudgingly, he returned the embrace. "I'm sorry; I should have told you where we were headed. I just...." He leaned back, and brushed the hair from Reece's brow in that now familiar, gentle gesture. "I just wanted to know you'd be okay tomorrow. I'll be thinking of you all day."

Reece sighed and pulled Ben back into a hug. Trust his cop to be looking out for him at every turn. "Let's go," he said quietly. "Through the park."

"You're sure?"

"I can't say I'm not going to be avoiding going through there whenever I can, it's only once in a blue moon my routes take me this far out anyway. But if I can jog through with you, I'm sure I'll be okay in the future."

Ben took his head in his hands and pressed a kiss to his brow, then rested his own forehead against his for a moment. "You're a strong guy, you know that? I admire you. I'm proud of you."

"Yeah well," Reece sighed, "you say that now. Just wait until you see me try to sprint."

Ben laughed and nodded over his shoulder. "Come on. I'll race you."

"I DO *not* look like a wounded water buffalo when I run!" Reece spluttered.

Ben threw back his head and laughed as they slowed back to a jog. They'd made it through the park, and had even taken a second lap. They'd raced the last lap through, and of course Ben had won.

"Let me say it again—get your ass on a bike, *then* we'll see who's faster!" Reece said, grinning. He bent at the waist and rested his hands on his knees while Ben stretched. He was a mess; Ben, of course, looked like an Adonis.

Ben was chuckling. He looked happy, relieved. "Walk it out a little, it'll help you cool down."

Reece followed him, and used the sleeve of his—of *Ben's* sweater to wipe his brow. He looked up to see Ben a few paces ahead of him, walking backward so he faced him—flashy bastard—with an odd smile on his face.

"What?"

Ben shook his head. "Those sleeves cover your hands," he said in a surprisingly soft voice.

"Well, you're huge. Of course the sweater's a little big on me."

Ben tilted his head and stopped walking. "I like how it looks on you."

Reece smiled, and looked down at himself. "Yeah? Well, in that case, I'm stealing it. You can't have it back."

Ben laughed. "Oh is that so?"

"Yes. I've run out of clothes again so I'm gonna have to either steal this, or go back to my place and…."

Ben frowned when he saw Reece flush. "What?"

"Ah, well, I guess I can go home." Reece stuffed his hands up into the sleeves and crossed his arms. He smiled with some embarrassment. "I mean, I'm all better now, aren't I? Those stairs shouldn't be a problem."

"Oh." The smile dropped from Ben's face. He licked his lips quickly and shrugged. "There's no rush, is there?"

Reece frowned. "No. But, well I'll have to go back eventually. Otherwise I'd just be hauling half my stuff back and forth all the time."

Ben stepped closer and placed his hands either side of Reece's neck. He looked Reece in the eyes, contemplating something. "What if you didn't?" he asked quietly.

"Didn't what?" Reece asked slowly, a nervous smile pulling at his lips. "God, Ben. Finish that sentence."

"What if you didn't go home, what if you lived with me?"

Reece couldn't help the blinding smile that crossed his lips, or the breathless, surprised laugh that escaped him. "You want to live with me?"

Seeing Reece smile like that—like he'd just made his day, his fucking *year*—Ben grinned in relief and stood close so that he could wrap his arms around Reece's neck and rest his brow against his. Reece's hands—still enveloped by those long sleeves—gripped loosely at the sides of Ben's sweater.

"Yes. I want to live with you. I want to see you every day. I want to cook for you, I want to crash on the couch watching old movies with you; I want to sleep with you every night."

"Ben," Reece gasped, and crushed his mouth to his. "Yes. Fucking *yes*. I'll live with you."

Ben smiled, so happy it was unreal. "Maybe we could even convert some of the spare rooms into a small studio for your work, or something?"

Reece's brows drew together in surprise, and he had to bite down on his lip hard to keep his smile from splitting his face in two. It was one of the most thoughtful of suggestions....

Ben laughed softly, and kissed Reece hard. "You make that house a home again, you know that?" he asked gruffly.

Reece swallowed around the lump in his throat and laughed in embarrassment as a tear escaped despite his best efforts to appear macho. "Aw, fuck," he said, sniffing, and wiped at the side of his face. "I'm going to love you until we're both old men. Did you know *that*?"

Ben grinned, then unwound his arms from Reece's neck and stepped back. "I have just one condition."

Reece blinked in surprise. "Okay, shoot."

"You never, I mean *never*, try to cook again."

Reece narrowed his eyes playfully and then grinned as he strolled closer to Ben. Ben gave him a suspicious look and backed up—right where Reece wanted him to.

"Okay, fine." And then he lunged.

He tackled Ben around the middle, and they both landed with a soft thud in the thick grass. As soon as he could breathe again, Ben started laughing. Reece straddled his middle, and held Ben's wrists down against the ground.

"I also have one stipulation."

"Shoot," Ben said.

"You keep your ludicrous-looking cat away from my fish."

CHAPTER 11

REECE couldn't help but laugh as Ben's hands covered his eyes and he was guided to sit at the kitchen table. When those hands lifted, he blinked a few times and then laughed at seeing the big chocolate cake sitting in front of him. It had a big 3-0 candle in the center, with little ones surrounding it.

"You made this, didn't you?" He looked back over his shoulder at Ben, who just shrugged in mock modesty.

Reece shook his head. He really hadn't been expecting this much of a fuss over his thirtieth. Ben had woken him up with a slow kiss and breakfast in bed. He'd gotten him a card and one small present which Reece had begrudgingly accepted despite their little deal over the bike, mainly because it had been so cute. It was a small Kermit doll. No guy had ever bought him a stuffed animal before—he'd always thought that kind of thing was for women, but Ben had been so adorable, just shrugging and smiling at him. Apparently he'd asked the store clerk for a Swedish chef, but when the clerk had looked at him like he was mad, he'd quickly asked for a Kermit instead. Well, they'd just *had* to have amazing birthday sex after that. Something that fucking adorable deserved a reaction.

Then he'd gone off to work as normal; they both had, or so he'd thought. When he got home—yes, *home*—this beautiful house was his home now, he'd nearly jumped out of his skin at the chorus of "Happy Birthday" that was yelled at him. He'd groaned but couldn't keep from smiling when he saw his friends laughing at him, complete with stupid party hats, no less.

Ben had taken the day off and had blown up balloons, baked a cake, and invited over their closest friends. Ted and Sharon were there, along with their kids, who were happily playing with Muddles. Roger was there, of course, along with Darren, and even his parents. If Ben had hired a magician or bouncy castle he wouldn't have been surprised.

He winced good-naturedly as they sang "Happy Birthday" off-key. There was a flash and he looked up and grinned at Darren, who was urging everyone to huddle in close so that he could get a picture of them all together. Reece reached behind him and took Ben's arms and wrapped them around himself so that Ben's lightly stubbled chin rested on his shoulder, and then smiled at the camera.

"Now make a wish and blow out your candles," Ben murmured and kissed his cheek.

"You know, I honestly can't think of single thing I need," he said with all sincerity. This was of course met with a groan and even gagging noises from Darren, making everyone laugh.

"Oh shut up," he said, laughing, and then took a deep breath and blew out the candles in one breath. Everyone cheered, and he felt himself flushing from all the attention. "I'm really wanting some of this cake." He dipped his finger in the edge of the icing and brought it to his lips with a satisfied hum.

Ben grinned. "You and food."

"Cake later, it's time for *presents*!" Darren clapped.

Reece laughed and shook his head. "You are so gay."

"Uh, yeah. Pot calling kettle black much?"

Before he could think of a witty reply, the cake was taken away—his eyes following it as it went—and colorfully wrapped gifts were set in front of him. He shook his head and laughed. "I can't believe you guys."

Witness

"Open ours first!" That was Amy, hopping excitedly.

He winked at the girls and unwrapped the small gift. He laughed in surprise and showed those crowding around close what it was. It was a black bell to go on his bike, and on top of it, it said in the "I heart NY" motif, "I heart my bike." He rang it and laughed.

"This is definitely going on my bike." He turned in his chair and held out his arms. They rushed to him and nearly knocked him out of his seat. "Thank you, ladies. Fashionable yet practical."

"Alright, ours next," Sharon announced.

Reece pulled at the ribbon of the neatly wrapped gift, and his brows rose in surprise. He held up a deep burgundy long-sleeved dress shirt.

"Oh, that's nice," his mother said, leaning against his father.

"Wow, guys, thanks."

"You'll have to wear it next time you go out." Sharon urged. Ted rolled his eyes at his wife's insistence.

Reece stood and held the shirt against his chest; he bet it'd fit like a glove and look classy too. "This is great, thank you, Sharon, Ted."

"The wife chose it, as if you couldn't guess. I wanted to get you beer."

Reece laughed and hugged Sharon, then Ted gave him a one-armed hug, patting him on the back.

"Can I give you my gift?" Roger piped up almost shyly around all the people he wasn't familiar with.

"Which one is it, Rog?" Ben asked.

"That one, the one wrapped in Christmas paper." Roger shot Reece a sheepish glance. "I wasn't wearing my glasses; I thought the snowmen were clowns."

Reece laughed affectionately. "Ain't nothing wrong with that."

"*Isn't*," his mother corrected, making Ben laugh.

Reece peeled away the Christmas paper, and held up a wooden box. He looked at Roger and then opened the box. Inside was an old chess board and pieces. The squares on the board were slightly faded, but the pieces, he realized, were made of some sort of stone. It was vintage, and classy.

"Wow, Rog, this is so cool!"

Roger, who had looked a little nervous, beamed happily at him. "I'm so glad you like it."

"And you know you're going to have to teach me how to play now, right?"

"I was counting on it."

Both Reece and Ben laughed at that. "Thanks, Rog, it's great."

Roger smiled. "You know I learned to play on that board, it belonged to my father."

Reece's smile faltered slightly in surprise. "You father's?" he asked quietly. "Oh, Rog, are you sure you want to give this to me?"

"Yes, of course." Roger glanced around in slight embarrassment, realizing he had become the focus of everyone's attention. He turned his mug of tea around in his hands. "You know, you were just a boy when you came to live in my block. All by yourself you were. Annabel"—he glanced quickly to those listening—"my late wife. Annabel and I liked you instantly. You were so polite and respectful, always paid your rent on time too!" he joked, and Reece laughed around the lump forming in his throat. "And, well, we never had any children of our own. And whether you knew it or not, Annabel always thought of you as a son. I know I certainly do." The old guy's chin began to tremble slightly. "It'd make me very happy if you'd take the board."

"Roger," Reece whispered, and stood to pull the guy into a tight hug.

"I sure am going to miss seeing you every day, Reece."

Witness

"Don't be silly." Reece gave a watery laugh, "You're going to be over here every week kicking my ass at chess, remember?"

Roger patted his back and spoke just as quietly, "I'll bring some beer."

A small choked-up whimper drew their attention over to Darren, who had his hand over his mouth, and his brows arched up sadly as he teared up. He met Reece's amused gaze and rolled his eyes. "I know, *so* gay." He waved his hand in front of his eyes. "Forgive me for not being made of stone."

He had everyone laughing; trust Darren to lighten the mood by making an ass of himself. Reece's mother gave him a tissue and hugged him. "Don't you listen to them," she said. "You've always been a sensitive boy."

That had Reece convulsing in laughter. Darren stuck his tongue out at him. Then Reece was forced to sit back down and open the rest of the presents. Darren bought him a Gorillapod. It was an adaptable, flexible tripod for point-and-shoot or SLR cameras. It could be wrapped around almost anything—trees, rocks, fences, anything—and gave a unique angle to any shot. He had to admit, it was pretty cool. It was certainly better than a goldfish.

His mom and dad had gotten him a subscription to a professional photography magazine, a new memory stick for his digital camera, and a picture collage clock. It was actually kind of awesome—the clock. It was a standard clock with small square metal frames surrounding it. He was already picking out which pictures of him and Ben he wanted in there. He hugged and kissed them both, thanked everyone again, and sighed in relief as the wrapping paper was cleared away, and the cake was brought back.

He touched Ben's elbow and kissed his cheek, whispering, "Thank you." Ben winked at him and cut into the cake. "You've actually got one more present, but I could see you eyeing the cake and getting hungrier by the second."

"Another present?" Reece asked around a mouthful of chocolate cake, and then he closed in eyes in bliss. "So good!"

"Just one, from me." Ben sat in the chair beside him, turning to face him, and handed him an envelope.

"Oh!" He heard Darren call from across the room where he'd gone to put on some music. "Wait for me, I want to watch!"

"*Ben*," he groused, taking the envelope. "We talked about this; the bike is my present, and Kermit."

"Kermit?" Darren asked, and then he rolled his eyes again. "You did *not* tell him about your weird Muppet obsession."

"He did. Saw it firsthand too. Scary stuff." Reece elbowed Ben in the side.

"Surely you've grown out of that by now, Reece." His father said.

Reece began to blush a little, and Ben laughed, rubbing his back. "Open the envelope, then you can have more cake."

He gave Ben a playful glare, and then opened the envelope. He frowned when he took out the Delta Airlines placard and gasped when he realized it held two tickets. Tickets to Iceland.

"Ben?" He looked at the man in shock. "You didn't...."

"I may have...."

"You—you bought me tickets to *fucking Iceland*?"

He heard Ted clear his throat and nod down at his two giggling nine-year-old girls. He instantly slapped his hand over his mouth. "Oh sh—uh. Sorry, girls. Ted, Sharon."

Luckily people were laughing, including the kids' parents, so he figured he wasn't in too much trouble. He turned his attention back to Ben, who was smiling. "Ben, I...." He stuttered over his words, too stunned to speak normally. " I can't believe you did this."

"Well, there are *two* tickets; I was planning on going with you." Ben leaned closer, rubbing his knee. "They're booked for late

September—fall. Apparently it's the best season to catch a glimpse of the Northern Lights."

Reece pressed his lips into a tight line. Too emotional to speak, he pushed back from the table, making the chair screech on the linoleum, and turned to wrap his arms around Ben's neck. "Ben," he whispered.

Ben crooned to him quietly and stood up, keeping Reece in his arms so that he could hug him properly. "I love you," he said quietly, for Reece alone to hear.

Reece pulled his head back from Ben's shoulder, relieved to see that everyone else had backed off a little to give them some privacy, though he did catch his mom and dad smiling at him.

He touched the side of Ben's face, kissing him softly. His hands drifted up and around Ben's neck, and Ben's arms settled at the small of his back and held him close. Without realizing it, they began to sway slightly to the music. Ben ducked his head for another kiss, and whispered to him with a boyish grin.

"You think they'd notice if we slipped away for a few minutes?"

Reece laughed quietly. "Probably." He craned his neck to whisper in Ben's ear. "I came up with a pretty inventive birthday wish."

"Oh yeah?"

"It involves you, me, and your handcuffs."

Ben coughed to hide the groan that rose in his throat. He couldn't hide the flush of arousal creeping up his neck, however. "I'm going to go to the pantry for some more wine. Perhaps you should excuse yourself and go to the bathroom?" he murmured huskily.

Reece grinned and watched Ben weave his way out of the kitchen. He waited for perhaps thirty seconds before excusing himself to the bathroom, and then met Ben in the hallway. He grabbed the man's hand and pulled him up the first few steps, and then nearly bowled over Darren, who was coming down the stairs.

Darren smiled. "Hey, you—" Then his eyes narrowed and he looked between them. Reece flushed red, and Darren rolled his eyes—something he'd done a lot of today—and stepped out of their way. "I'll make something up if they ask. I wouldn't be too long if I were you. Or noisy," he said, chuckling.

Ben winked at Darren and pushed Reece up the stairs. Reece had just gotten the bedroom door closed when Ben pushed him back against it. His mouth crashed down hot against Reece's, and Reece gasped as the T-shirt he'd been wearing was whipped off over his head. Ben's mouth sought his again as he pulled at the buttons of Reece's jeans, shoving them quickly down his legs.

"Christ," Reece said, laughing breathlessly.

"Shh," Ben murmured, leaving him for only a second to grab some lube.

Reece pulled at the button and zip to Ben's jeans, and then shoved them down his thighs. He gasped when Ben took him by the back of the thighs and lifted him clear off of his feet and slammed him back against the door.

"Wrap your legs around my waist," Ben growled.

Managing to hold Reece against the door with one arm and his body, he ripped the foil wrapper he'd picked up along with the lube and quickly rolled on the condom. He spread the lube messily over his dick.

"Don't bother with me, just do it."

Ben hesitated. "Sure?"

"God, yes, we gotta be quick or they'll notice we're gone."

Ben pulled Reece's legs tighter around him and lined himself up before pushing into Reece steadily. Reece only winced a little, but was otherwise in heaven. He gripped onto Ben's strong, broad shoulders and squeezed his eyes shut in bliss as Ben began to thrust into him hard and fast.

"Oh, fuck, Ben…." he moaned.

Witness

Ben's hand came up quickly to cover his mouth, just turning him on all the more. Reece could only close his eyes and hang on as Ben fucked him hard and fast.

"Shit," Ben growled in a low, guttural voice.

Reece let out a helpless cry behind Ben's hand, and came between them, all over Ben's T-shirt. Ben followed him only seconds later, gritting his teeth and growling obscenities that made Reece grin proudly and raise an eyebrow in surprise. They both rode the waves for a few moments, and then Ben gently lowered Reece's legs back onto the ground.

Reece rested his brow against Ben's shoulder, getting his breath back, and then they parted with sheepish grins. "Well, well. Officer Jenkins, you do surprise me."

Ben laughed and peeled off his T-shirt. "Just you wait 'til tonight. You wished for handcuffs, you're getting them."

Reece's smile was both delighted and surprised. "Holy shit. You're a dream, a wet fucking dream come true." He laughed and tugged his jeans back on.

Ben handed him his already dirtied T-shirt, and Reece quickly wiped himself down and sprayed on some deodorant. Both dressed. They didn't know if they should be smug or embarrassed that they'd only been gone for five minutes or so. They went back down and at the bottom of the stairs Ben patted his behind in the direction of the kitchen.

"I probably should go find some wine. You go on back in there, enjoy your party."

"I still can't believe you did all this for me."

"Thirty's a milestone, remember?"

A decidedly tender look crossed Reece's features. "Yeah, I remember." He pulled Ben forward for a gentle but by no means chaste kiss, whispered another thank you, and went back to the party.

TED and Sharon had been the first to leave. Amy and Tracey had started to blink sleepily, and Muddles could only entertain two nine-year-olds for so long. Darren had driven Roger home, and his parents had gone to stay in a hotel, despite Ben offering them the guest room. He was glad his parents had declined, sensing that perhaps it would be best for them not to be around while Reece and Ben christened the house. Still, they were coming back over tomorrow for lunch before heading home.

Reece had moved in two weeks ago, but there were still boxes waiting to be unpacked. He'd stayed at Ben's ever since he'd been asked to move in, but had only actually moved his possessions over a couple of weeks ago due to excessive laziness on both their parts. He'd been getting back into the swing of things with work, and his month away had not left him unfit, but did at least make him realize how fit he usually was. Ben had been getting to know his new partner a little better—Officer Carl Brown—the guy who had taken Reece's statement in the hospital. He'd been invited to the party apparently, but hadn't been able to make it. They'd arranged to have Carl over a night after work anyhow.

Reece sighed. A bike, a party, plane tickets. Try as he might, he couldn't ignore the nagging feeling that he couldn't accept it all. It was too much. He didn't know how to compensate for all the consideration, all the loving gestures Ben had shown him. He, himself, did not feel equal to it. He didn't know how to carry on while believing that he wasn't enough—that he wasn't equal to this amazing man that loved him.

"This one has to go in the bedroom."

Reece glanced up from the box of books he had opened when Ben held up the framed photo he'd taken of a couple of starfish on a beach. It didn't sound too amazing, but he'd kind of liked it and had developed it in black and white. He'd waited until sunset, and taken a low shot so he'd have an amazing view of the horizon behind. He'd always thought that shot had been a little romantic of him. He smiled.

"Yeah, you're right. Though, you know you don't have to put up all my work, right?" He laughed. "I don't want to completely take over."

"It's not you taking over; it's me appreciating a piece of art."

Reece smiled and shook his head. He didn't know why, but coming from Ben, and not his parents or friends, it meant the absolute world to him.

They'd mostly cleaned up from the party now, and were attempting to tackle at least a few boxes before they went to bed and screwed each other silly. Though Ben's promise of handcuffs wasn't helping him get anything done. Christ, the man would even cuff him up if he asked him to.

"Ben," Reeve began hesitantly. "About those plane tickets...."

Ben grinned at him proudly. "You excited?"

"It was... the most thoughtful, *amazing* gift. But, um...."

"But?" Ben asked with a frown.

"Ben, I can't accept them. You should get your money back."

"What?" Ben laughed, giving him a silly smile. "You've always wanted to go to Iceland. To take pictures of 'nature at its most spectacular'?"

"Right, and I still do, but...." He bit his lip. The last thing he wanted to do was hurt Ben's feelings. "Ben, it's too much. I couldn't possibly... after all you've done for me? I can't—"

"Whoa." Ben held his hands up. "What's going on, you want to go but don't feel you can accept?"

"Yes."

Ben raised one eyebrow. "Reece, that's bullshit."

Reece blinked at Ben in surprise. "How is it bullshit?"

"Because you want it and I'm trying to give it to you, you don't have to be polite and decline—"

"I'm not. Honestly. We just"—he was getting frustrated, and gestured between the two of them—"I love you and I'm going to make this last, but it has to be even. You deserve better and I should be able to give you it. I'm thirty and if I can just get my business going and—"

"Hey," Ben said gently, walking over to Reece and holding him by the arms. "What is this really about?"

Reece sighed. "I didn't earn this house. I'd still be living in my tiny apartment at thirty if it wasn't for you."

"Reece, I didn't earn this house, either. I inherited it. You don't think I'd be in exactly the same place you were a few weeks ago if my father hadn't left this place to me when he died?" His lips lifted at the corner of his mouth. "I'm a cop. We don't earn that much."

"I just want to be better. More than I am. Not just for myself anymore, though, but for you too. It's just hard to keep up with everything when you're so good to me. I know that sounds ridiculous."

Ben frowned, as if trying to remember something. "We've spoken about this before, haven't we? You have this thing about not being everything you feel you could be, even though you have all the time in the world right now. Why is that? Why do you—"

Reece pulled his arm away with a sigh. He didn't whip it away in a tantrum, he just needed to step back and order his thoughts. He bumped into the box he'd been unpacking, and his books tumbled at his and Ben's feet.

"Shit."

Ben sighed and helped him pick the books up. He turned and picked the last one up behind him. A plain black book. Ben frowned; it had no title or image on the front. Something skittered from between the pages and he bent to pick up what he thought at first was one of the pages come loose. He turned the paper over and stopped still.

"What's this?"

Witness

"Hmm?" Reece looked at what Ben held, and his cheeks flushed. "Oh."

It was a newspaper clipping of an officer pulling a man off of a ledge and back into a building. It was an image of Ben from months before, when he'd pulled back the jumper; the incident had caused quite a scene that day, and had gotten onto the news, and apparently, in the papers.

"That's, um... it's a clipping."

"Of me?" Ben asked gently.

Reece sighed and lowered his gaze, taking the clipping from him. "I went out and got a paper the next day." He looked up and shrugged sheepishly. "I was proud of you."

Ben's brows arched together and he smiled sadly. He took Reece by his elbows. "And you seriously can't see what it is you do for me? I've got friends, Reece; I've got some real close friends like Ted and Sharon who are like family. But then I've got you, and you trump them all. No, you're not everything you want to be, *yet*. But don't think for a second that you're not enough for me."

Reece sighed, and Ben could see, with some frustration, that he wasn't getting through to him. He frowned. "What happened to make you feel this way?" he asked quietly, and apparently hit a nerve because Reece tried to pull away again. The action made Ben drop the book.

He let go of Reece and picked the book up again. He flicked briefly through the pages, and then it dawned on him that he wasn't holding a store-bought book. The pages contained handwriting, not printed text.

"It's a journal."

Ben looked up when he heard Reece whisper, and was surprised at the sudden lack of color in his face. Reece met his gaze and swallowed hard. His jaw clenched, and he seemed to be gathering his courage. "You want to know why?"

Ben nodded. "Tell me. You can tell me anything."

Reece shook his head, letting out a humorless laugh. When he met Ben's gaze next, it was with tears in his eyes. "Please don't think less of me," he whispered desperately, "I don't think I could stand it if you did."

"God, Reece." His hands went straight for Reece's face, cupping it gently. He hunched his shoulders and kissed him gently and reassuringly. "Nothing could do that. Baby, talk to me about this. It's eating you up."

Reece swallowed, getting his voice under control. "That journal?"

Ben's thumbs rubbed gently over his cheekbones, "Yeah?"

"It was my dad's idea. After the accident, I had problems with my short-term memory. I'm fine now, but I haven't been able to kick the habit of making lists."

"Lists?"

Reece nodded, "I don't do it every day, not even every week. But every now and again I'll test myself. Just sit and make a list of everything I've done over the past few days, just to see if I remember it all."

"I don't understand."

Reece gently touched Ben's wrists, and lowered the man's gentle touch away from his face. "I was in a coma. When I woke up, my memory was hazy and took a while to align itself in my mind."

"Wait." Ben's eyes widened, suddenly hearing everything Reece was saying. "You were *in* the accident?" Ben asked softly. "The one with... your brother?"

Reece squeezed his eyes shut for a minute and swallowed hard. "Please don't get mad, I know I didn't tell you—"

Ben immediately shook his head. "Forget it, if you kept something from me I know it was with good reason. It's okay, go on...."

Reece sighed, and forced himself to look into those blue eyes filled with confusion. "I was driving the car."

"Oh," Ben gasped, compassion overwhelming him. "Reece...." A lot of things began to slowly fall into place. Reece didn't drive, not because he couldn't legally, but because he couldn't physically make himself. He hadn't mentioned his brother at the start of their relationship when he'd asked, not just out of grief over a lost brother, but out of grief and *guilt*.

"I was driving the car that killed my brother," Reece gasped, and then he choked on a sob trying to make its way out of his throat.

"Reece." Ben pulled in straight into his arms and held him tight. "God, what you must have gone through. I'm so sorry." He eased Reece's head to his shoulder and just held onto him.

Reece let out a pitiful little laugh, but didn't move. "That was their reaction, Mom and Dad's. No one got mad at me. I wish they had."

"Can you tell me what happened, in the accident?"

Reece sighed, and turned his head to the side to rest his cheek against Ben's shoulder. "Some guy ran a red light. Plowed right into the passenger side door, where Ryan was. The car—the one I was driving, slammed into a telephone pole. Then everything was black. The last thing I remember is hearing Ryan gasp." He closed his eyes tightly and clenched his jaw. "I woke up nearly four weeks later." He gripped Ben's T-shirt tightly in his fists, and whispered, "They'd already had Ryan's funeral."

"Christ," Ben breathed, gently rubbing Reece's back. "I can't even imagine... you were what? Eighteen?"

Reece nodded. "I left home a year later, came out here. Scared my parents, but I just couldn't be there anymore."

"I know you don't need me to tell you that it wasn't your fault. You must have heard that again and again from your parents, from Darren?"

Reece nodded. "I know logically it wasn't my fault. But... I'd only had my license a few days; I kept thinking that if I'd only been able to get control of the car when we were hit...."

Ben shook his head, his voice was firm. "No. You know better than that. Not one part of that accident was your fault."

"I could barely look at my parents. Ryan...." Reece groaned and buried his face in Ben's T-shirt again.

"Shh, it's alright. You can tell me."

"He was my best friend, Ben. God, I loved my big brother. You know, he was the one who encouraged me with my photography. And he was the first person I told I was gay." He let out a weak laugh suddenly. "You know what he said?"

"Tell me."

"He said, 'That's fucking gross, Reece, but whatever'."

Ben frowned but couldn't help smiling a little. Reece pulled back his head to look Ben in the eye; Ben's heart broke a little at the sadness he saw there.

"It was the best response I could have asked for. My parents, they were never cruel or angry. They accepted it, but it threw them, they didn't know what to do with it."

"Whereas Ryan offered you his indifference." Ben nodded.

Reece actually smiled a little. "He even asked me if I was seeing anyone, as easy as anything. As if we were talking about girls."

"He sounds like he was a good guy."

"You've no idea. God, Ben, he was... he was smart, athletic; he was fucking straight up with everyone. I mean it. You could be anyone in the world, and he'd stop and give you the time of day, he looked out for me every day of my life. And he died. He was twenty years old and he died. He could have been anything! He could do anything but he just disappeared! I woke up and he was gone, just fucking...." he trailed

Witness

off, words becoming too difficult as he ground his teeth and squeezed his eyes shut.

"Oh, Reece," Ben sighed sadly. "Shit. I get it."

Reece let out a harsh breath. "I know. I expect too much from myself, like I'm trying to punish myself for what happened. I've heard it before, Ben." His words were more defeated than angry.

Ben lifted Reece's chin up and held it there. "I think it's more than that." Reece frowned, and Ben continued delicately. "It's like you've gotten it into your head that you have to make up for his absence. You think you have to compensate for everything he could have been, don't you? You hold him so high in your esteem"—he cut Reece off before he could argue—"and rightly so, that you've given yourself impossible standards to reach. Especially when it comes to me—to think you have to be more before you can accept a gift from me?"

Reece sighed and shook his head. But Ben wouldn't let him look or pull away. "No, I'm not going to criticize or get frustrated with you for it. But I am going to try and make you see it for what it is. Reece, you're not responsible for what happened, how could you be? Neither are you accountable for the pain his not being there has caused anyone else." He brushed the pads of his thumbs gently over Reece's cheekbones.

"I'm not so stupid as to think that I can change the way you've been thinking and feeling over the past eleven years in an instant. But I can tell you this, I'll spend every day of the rest of my life trying to convince you that everything you are, everything you do and achieve—" He shrugged helplessly. "It's enough. *You* are enough." He swallowed hard. "You're an incredible man." A thought seemed to occur to him. "You're like your brother."

"Don't say that," Reece breathed, closing his eyes tight.

"No, you look at me," Ben held his chin gently, his thumb touching just under his lip. "You say your brother's smart, that he's kind. That he'd give the time of day to anyone? What does that make you?"

"Don't, it's not like that," Reece said sadly.

"So you're not the man who slept on an old man's couch for weeks, just so that someone would be there to look after him? Be there for him when he woke up in the middle of the night, confused, lost...." He winced and said softly, "crying?" Ben shook his head. "Do you know how proud that makes me to be the person you choose? That someone as compassionate and kind as that wants to be with me?"

Reece said nothing, but watched Ben, listening to him.

Ben touched his cheek gently. "I am so in love with you it fucking hurts, Reece." His voice was low, strained. "So for you to turn that away, turn away any gesture of mine, to think I'm *wrong* for loving you as you are—then you're doing me a disservice."

"I never meant...." Reece whispered, taken aback by all Ben had said.

Ben nodded. "I know. And it's alright, I swear it is." He gently brushed the hair away from Reece's brow as he picked his words carefully. "But do you really think that Ryan would want you to lead your life with his death constantly overshadowing it?"

How many times had his parents or Darren tried to say something similar? They'd never put it quite so bluntly, probably afraid of him running away again, but it had never really hit home like this. Perhaps it wasn't as easy to accept coming from his parents or Darren because they had known him before the accident, and they had known Ryan. And while he couldn't say Ben had a completely objective view, he was the only one who could say what he'd said without it hurting him, because he *hadn't* known Ryan—he didn't know what it was to lose him, but he *did* know what it was to lose one of the people you loved most.

Reece slowly pulled Ben against him, frowning as his arms wound around his middle. "I haven't been very fair to you," he said quietly. "Have I?"

Ben sighed and rested his cheek against Reece's temple and rubbed his back. "I don't think it's a question of fair. You might not have been as open with me as you could have, but that's alright, it's okay that you kept a little bit of yourself back. As long as you know that you don't need to. As long as you *know* that you deserve everything good that happens to you, and that you don't have to punish yourself for not being more than you need to be."

"Ben?"

"Yeah?"

"You know this is going to stay with me my entire life, right? My family's been telling me all this shit for the past ten years and none of it's sunk in."

"As long as you can start to believe what I'm saying, it doesn't matter how long it takes you."

"You can deal?" he whispered.

"I'm not going anywhere."

Reece nodded, and wiped at his cheeks with his sleeve. He managed a small smile. "Christ, how many fucking times am I going to cry in front of you?"

Ben laughed and crushed Reece to him. "Come on, you haven't really, you've been either injured or ambushed by sentimentality. Don't worry, your manhood is intact."

"Okay, then." Reece sighed and looked around at the boxes. "There's something you should know about me."

"What's that?"

"Asides from not being able to cook, I'm messy as hell."

Ben snorted and shook his head. "You're not too bad."

"No, really. I've been making an effort so far. I'm actually a complete slob."

"You want to leave all this crap for tomorrow?"

"God, yes."

Ben smiled and then reached down to give Reece a toe-curling kiss, making him moan helplessly. "There's something you should know too," Ben murmured.

"At this point you could tell me anything and I wouldn't care."

Ben's hands slid down to squeeze Reece's behind. "I'm taking you to Iceland whether you like it or not. You are going to see those lights."

Reece laughed and linked his arms back around Ben's neck. "Thank you for my party," he whispered against Ben's lips. "Thank you for everything."

Leaving the unpacked boxes behind, Ben lead Reece upstairs, only to dash down a few minutes later to look for his handcuffs.

Chapter 12

REECE had told him once that taking pictures was a small window into another person's life, his way of witnessing just a small part of it. A completely bare and honest glimpse into that someone's heart. While Ben had thought the words very eloquent, he'd never really been able to understand the meaning behind them. Not until now.

The tickets to Iceland had been expensive, but the expression on Reece's face, the *awe* there, was priceless. Lights danced across the sky, and it was indeed beautiful, but if he had to choose between the lights and Reece's choked-up expression, he'd never look away from Reece again.

Ben moved to stand behind him, wrapping his arms around him, just holding him close as they looked up. Reece held his camera in his hands, but made no move to take a shot. Their breath puffed in front of them, and he could just make out the pink tip of Reece's nose in the low light. He could feel Reece's shuddering breath.

"Not going to take a picture?" he asked gently.

Reece swallowed and gave a little laugh. For once he didn't care that his emotions were so obvious. No one was near but Ben, which just made it all the more special.

"I'm not sure I could do it justice," he answered quietly.

"It is beautiful, but I'm sure you could."

"No, more than beautiful." Reece shook his head, unable to tear his gaze away from the sky. His voice had a slight warble to it. "You know, I'm not the most spiritual of people, I never took to it much...." He swallowed, and continued in a near whisper, "But I reckon if there is a heaven somewhere, then that's a slice of it right there in front of us."

Reece hadn't realized that a tear had escaped until Ben's gloved hand brushed his cheek. He rolled his eyes at himself and laughed. "Shit." He turned his head away from Ben to wipe his cheek, but Ben turned him in his arms.

"This right here?" Ben touched the damp trail on his cheek. "That's what makes you so good at what you do."

Reece smiled, turned his face into Ben's palm and closed his eyes for a moment, before pulling Ben close by the front of his jacket and kissing him. Ben hummed into the kiss, thinking that he had never been more content in his life. He smiled as Reece pulled away from the kiss with a quiet laugh.

"What?" he asked with a chuckle.

Reece stretched his neck and kissed the tip of his nose. "Your nose is cold."

"Sap," Ben accused affectionately.

Reece pushed Ben back, pointing behind him. "Stand there." He sniffed; it was damn cold. "If I'm taking pictures they're going to be family album pictures, just for us."

Ben stood where he was told, stuffed his hands into his thick jacket and smiled. Reece took a few shots, telling him where to stand and even going to his knees for one shot to have the lights right over Ben's head.

"That one's going in my wallet." Reece narrowed his eyes in thought for a second, and then grinned mischievously. "Along with a few others, perhaps."

Ben laughed, and actually felt himself flush a little despite the cold. Reece had gotten pretty inventive with his camera earlier when he caught Ben just as he was leaving the shower.

Witness

"Give me that." Ben gestured for the camera, and laughed when Reece posed with his arms outstretched and a cheesy grin on his lips. "You are such a tourist," he said. "Want to go get some grub before we call it a day?"

"Yeah." Reece looked up at the sky, and sighed again. "Thank you for bringing me here." He looked at Ben. "I never would have seen any of this if it weren't for you."

Ben shook his head, pocketing the camera. "I don't know about that. I figure you would have made it here eventually. You're hardy like that."

"Hardy?" Reece laughed in surprise.

"Yeah, hardy." Ben grinned boyishly, and took Reece's hand as they began to walk.

"Maybe. I'm thinking that seeing it with you makes all the difference, though."

THEY'D rented a small apartment in Reykjavik: bedroom, bathroom, sitting area with cozy fireplace, and a kitchen. Ben walked in, shucked his jacket and flipped on the light. He turned in surprise when Reece flipped the switch back off.

"What are you up to?" As if he didn't know.

Reece kicked off his shoes and placed his jacket over the back of a chair. He said nothing, simply took Ben's hand and led him to the bedroom. Ben's hand went for the light switch out of habit—that's just what you did when you entered a dark room. But Reece's soft but firm "no" stopped him.

Ben felt his pulse begin to quicken at the husky note in Reece's voice, and wet his bottom lip unconsciously as Reece slowly pushed him to lie back on the bed. The room was dark, but they had a balcony that let in any moon or star light. He watched as Reece pulled his sweater over his head as he went to pull back the light curtain. He heard

Reece let out an astonished little laugh, and nearly gasped as Reece stood aside to show him. Ben leaned up on his elbows and uttered an impressed "wow" as the shades of green danced against the ceiling like waves.

Reece moved back into his line of vision, and he laid back down, watching as Reece stripped for him. He said a quiet "hi" as Reece kneeled on the bed, pulling the shirt over Ben's head and kissing him with a small smile in return. He hummed softly in anticipation as Reece pulled down his khakis and underwear, aroused as hell when Reece straddled his legs, both of them naked, and bent his head over Ben's groin.

He liked it when Reece took his time, just loving his body with that mouth. But there was also something to be said for when the guy just went straight for his dick. Like he couldn't wait and just had to have it in his mouth. Ben fucking loved that. He groaned and bent his knees a little as Reece's hands gripped his hips, his head bobbing up and down on Ben's cock, sucking on him.

"Christ... that mouth," Ben groaned.

Reece pulled off of his cock with a wet pop and crawled up the length of Ben's body to straddle his hips. He kissed Ben as he leaned down to reach for the lube under the pillow, then pulled back and flipped the cap open to coat his fingers. Ben wasn't sure what to expect—who would be doing the fucking—not until Reece reached around to stretch himself. Ben moaned loudly and gripped Reece's thighs tightly.

He bit his lip hard as he helped Reece impale himself until his backside was touching his balls. And it was a sight to behold as Reece began to slowly move on his cock. Just up and down, grinding and squeezing. Reece's hands searched for his, and their fingers entwined as Reece's movements became quicker, with a hint of desperation.

Reece snatched his hands quickly from Ben's and planted them just above each of his muscular shoulders as he moved faster on Ben's dick. Ben's hands went straight to his hips, helping him.

"Yes," Ben hissed.

"Fuck, oh fuck...." Reece began that quiet stream of profanity that Ben loved so much, showing how much he was enjoying Ben having his ass. Ben ground his teeth, growling out that he loved him, and when he couldn't take it anymore, he pushed up in a quick move and had Reece on his back.

Reece gasped in excitement and then moaned helplessly, wantonly, as Ben spread his thighs wide apart and demanded they wrap around his waist. He loved it when Ben got so desperately turned on that he'd just take over, take from Reece exactly what he wanted, blowing his mind in the process.

"Yeah Ben, just like... *ah*! That, there, right... *there*."

"You like that?" Ben growled, thrusting balls-deep.

"God, yes. Fuck me," he panted. "Give it to me. Give it to me baby...."

A hand wound its way into Reece's hair, gripping almost painfully tight as their mouths crashed together.

"Fuck, Reece. Reece...." Ben moaned.

"Everything, Ben. You're fucking"—he gasped sharply—"everything to me."

Ben pushed up on his hands with a roar and just let rip on Reece, giving him everything. Reece's breath escaped from his lungs, and his hands had to brace above him on the headboard to keep himself from crashing into it with every thrust. Ben had never fucked him this hard, and he could only whimper as Ben took his ass, just spread him wide and owned it.

Reece would think later that he was especially glad that they were in a rented apartment and not a hotel. The headboard was banging against the wall; the scream that left him as he came was something he'd never thought he'd hear come from his own mouth. And the guttural, animalistic cry that left Ben was almost enough to excite him all over again.

Ben collapsed on top of him, his face buried in Reece's neck as Reece clutched at his slick back. They panted harsh breaths, and Reece pressed his lips to one damp, broad shoulder as their heartbeats slowly began to return to normal. He ran his fingers through the hair at the nape of Ben's neck that was wringing wet, and just held the heavy form to him as they both wound down from their high.

"My God," Reece said breathlessly, one arm still wrapped around Ben as his free hand ran through his own damp hair. "Where the fuck did that come from, huh, stud?" He laughed.

Ben only hummed and turned his face to kiss Reece's neck, not yet ready to move. "Guess you brought it out of me." His voice was hoarse and still deep.

Reece chuckled quietly, the stubble on Ben's cheeks tickling. "Shit, I've never been fucked like that in all my life. Jesus."

Ben finally lifted himself up with a groan, giving Reece a deep kiss that caught him by surprise, before holding the edge of the condom and slowly pulling out. "Ah, shit."

"What?"

"It split again."

"Well, what do you expect with that monster dick between your thighs there?"

Ben laughed and sat on the side of the bed as he peeled the latex off, then headed to the bathroom. On the bed, lying there with his thighs apart, slick with sweat and his own come, Reece was still feeling slightly dazed. Ben came back into the bedroom but halted by the bed, just looking at him. "Fuck," he breathed. His hand reaching for his dick as it unbelievably twitched. "Look at you."

Reece hummed in satisfaction, one arm resting above his head and the other on his stomach, idly making swirling patterns in the dampness there. One of his knees bent and the other lay flat, leaving himself open. He looked at Ben with those dark eyes of his. "Like what you see?" he asked, not even guessing the half of it.

Witness

"You're the most beautiful man I've ever known, I fucking swear to God."

Reece's eyebrow quirked at the earnestness in Ben's voice, and he choked out a little laugh in surprise, seeing Ben's dick begin to rise again in his hand. "Well, shit," he said breathlessly, lowering the arm that rested above his head and then lifting up on his elbows. He bent both knees slightly, and let his legs fall as far apart as they could. His voice was lower and seductive when he spoke. "Maybe you'd better lay yourself back between my thighs and have another go."

Ben groaned and squeezed his cock before doing exactly as suggested, climbing back over Reece. "Love it when you talk like a slut for me," he growled into Reece's ear, his hands just caressing wherever they could reach.

Reece laughed again in surprise, more excited by those words than he dared admit. He arched his back slightly, wrapping his legs around Ben's waist again before biting his lip and whispering into his ear words that seemed a little out there even for him: "Only a slut for you. Let you do what the fuck you want with me, I'm all yours."

Ben groaned loudly. "Now I gotta have you again." He'd been kissing along Reece's neck, stroking the sides of those thighs as they wrapped tightly around him, but he paused a second, and pulled back far enough to look Reece in the eye. His voice was soft and a touch uncertain. "How'd you feel about losing the latex?"

Reece blinked in surprise, his heart speeding up. "You mean now?"

Ben shrugged, starting to thrust lazily against him. "You got tested after that first time, when the condom split, didn't you?"

The corner of Reece's lips tugged up in the beginnings of a grin. "Yeah."

Ben grinned right back. "Well I got test results back not two weeks ago. A work thing. So that makes us…?"

"Good to go." Reece smiled nervously, then nodded his head. "Yeah. Yeah, do it." He watched Ben as he arched his back again.

"You want me with nothing between, you got it. I'll give you anything I can, Ben. I mean it."

Ben growled, knowing that it excited his lover when he did, and licked across Reece's lips. "You'd let me fuck you bareback?"

Just the words excited him. "Yes," Reece answered in a shuddering breath. "I love you, fucking trust you with my life."

"Oh God," Ben gasped. "You still good from before?"

Reece nodded, excitement zinging through him. "Just slip it in me."

"Get me back up. I'm nearly there." Ben put Reece's hand over his almost fully erect cock, encouraging him to stroke. "You're remarkably good for my recovery time," he said, laughing breathlessly.

Reece brought him back to full arousal, and Ben watched Reece closely as he pushed slowly inside. The feeling was incredible. It felt tighter, and so, *so* much hotter. He'd had no idea the warmth the latex had kept out, and he groaned loudly as he slid all the way inside Reece's body. He watched Reece, watched him close his eyes as his mouth slowly fell open, listened to him pant harshly.

"Oh God," Reece gasped, opening his eyes and staring right into equally as astonished blue eyes. "I had no idea, oh God."

Ben laughed, and was fascinated as it made Reece flinch. "Did you feel that?"

Reece smiled shakily and nodded his head. "I can't wait to feel you come inside of me, I want to feel it so bad."

Ben groaned, and felt his balls draw up at the thought of it. "Baby, this is going to be short."

"Don't care, just do it." Reece lifted his hips. "Please, Ben."

It was almost leisurely this time. The frenzy that had overtaken them before was replaced by an intensely slow and deep rhythm. The feel of Reece undulating beneath him, panting like an animal against his lips as they kissed, was one of the most seductive and beautiful things Ben had ever felt. He growled low in his throat and hid his face against Reece's neck as his thrusts became sharper, drawing little cries of shock from Reece as he reached down to squeeze Ben's clenching cheeks in his hands, trying to push him in deeper.

Reece's orgasm took Ben by surprise. Heat splashed between them, and that tight, steaming hot glove around his dick clenched. With a helpless groan, Ben jerked and came inside of Reece in hard spurts. He heard Reece gasp, and had to pull his head back to look at the man's expression. It was one of surprise and pleasure.

"You came inside of me," Reece whispered.

"I did." He kissed Reece slowly, deeply, before pushing up on his arms and slowly pulling out. "I gotta see it." He pushed Reece's knees back gently and groaned in what sounded like agony when he saw his spunk dribbling out of Reece's hole. "That's fucking amazing. We are so doing that again."

When Reece's eyebrows shot up in disbelief, Ben actually laughed. "No baby, I'm thirty-five, not twenty-five. I meant next time."

Reece smiled and then sighed in what sounded like sated exhaustion. "It was incredible."

"Yeah, it was. You were." Ben lay down beside Reece, pulling him into his arms.

Reece smiled suddenly, blindingly, and reached up to pull Ben's face to his with both hands, kissing him soundly. "I love you."

"I know, baby."

"I think...." Reece frowned.

"What? You okay?"

"I think I need a shower."

Ben laughed. "Why don't I run you a bath? I could sneak in there with you. I'll even put bubbles in it."

Reece hummed happily. "You mind if I stay here while you do it?"

"Yeah, sure." Ben kissed him before getting off of the bed.

"I'm worried I might drip," Reece admitted with a flush, and Ben laughed.

"You stay put."

Ben filled the tub with warm water and even bubbles and then went back to the bed just as Reece was yawning and sitting up—it was late and he was beginning to flag, himself. Before the man could even get a word out, Ben swooped in and hooked his arms behind his knees and back, swinging Reece up against him. He laughed as Reece squawked in surprise and quickly wrapped his arms around Ben's neck.

"Geez," he said, laughing, "warn a guy, would you?"

Ben carried him into the bathroom, and murmured to him in a teasing voice, "Don't want you dripping, now do we?"

"Oh Christ," Reece said, resting his brow against Ben's neck.

"You go ahead and get settled." He put Reece on his feet so that he could climb into the bath. "I'm going to change the sheets so we can climb right into bed after."

Reece sighed as he settled into the hot water. "Thanks, this feels so good. Why don't you just dump the sheets on the floor and get a duvet from the cupboard? Want to scrub your back."

Reece watched Ben leave the bathroom, and then he splashed water over his face, trying to erase the stupid grin that was there. He felt so good.

EPILOGUE

REECE smiled and he stood back to listen to Ben and his father discuss bait—or something fishing related—as they stood side by side, rods in hand. They'd come to visit his parents for their thirty-fifth wedding anniversary. His mom and dad held a small get-together at the house. Their oldest friends, his aunts and cousins had all been there, and he'd been as proud as anything as his mom introduced Ben to everyone, and that Ben had just indulged her with a kind smile. She's been particularly delighted with the lemon tart Ben had baked and brought along. As it was, she was lucky there was a tart at all—it had taken all his willpower not to eat it in the car ride over.

Cuter still was his father's excitement at whisking his "two boys" away to his favorite fishing hole afterwards. Initially, he'd felt a pang of sadness to hear his father refer to them both as his boys—it was always what he'd called Ryan and him. But with one look at Ben and the touched expression on his face, the sadness left him, and was replaced by a feeling of wellbeing. Something he never thought he could have when thinking of his brother.

Usually it was just him and his dad. He wasn't a fan of fishing, but enjoyed the time alone with his father. Well, now he could spend time with his dad, but having Ben there meant he didn't have to fish. So he'd brought along his camera and was content to look for the occasional good shot, or to just take pictures of his dad or Ben. So far he hadn't managed to get a good one of them together. He was just waiting for a lull in their conversation to get one, but was hesitant to interrupt their bonding—it was fucking adorable.

"What rod did your father use?" his dad asked Ben.

"He always liked the All Star rod, said it gave a great casting distance. I always liked the Shakespeare Ugly stick, it has good sensitivity…."

Seeing that the lull he was waiting for wasn't coming any time soon, he cleared his throat. "Guys, sorry to interrupt, but do you think I could get one of the two of you together?" He held up his camera.

"Sure." His father set down his rod. "Come here, son." He put his arm around Ben's shoulder, and there it was—the perfect picture. He always strove for that open shot, emotions laid bare. And that's what he was looking at. Whether his father knew it or not, those few words had meant the world to Ben. *"Come here, son."*

He could see emotions play over Ben's face—the pride and acceptance, the touch of sadness, but mostly, there was gratitude. Reece gave him a quick wink before raising the camera to his eye and taking the shot.

"Got it," he said softly.

L.A. GILBERT currently lives in a small British town where not much of anything ever really occurs. Jumping from job to job, she has no real qualifications in anything and is blithely proud of it. Between spectacularly failing driving test after test, she generally spends her free time reading about beautiful gay men, if not attempting to write about them. She is perhaps not the most outgoing of people, but is certainly one of the most cheerful.

Her aspirations are to eventually leave England and see a real, live whale (London's zoo is poorly lacking in that respect) and to perhaps one day hold in her hands a published copy of her own work.

One down.

Contemporary Romance from DREAMSPINNER PRESS

BROKEN
Dawn Kimberly Johnson

THE ONE THAT GOT AWAY
Rhianne Aile • Madeleine Urban

Marie Sexton
PROMISES

Wes & Toren
J.M. Colail

http://www.dreamspinnerpress.com